Praise for

Men of Phuket: Tongue Thai'd

Tongue Thai'd is a very visual and fast moving story about two very colorful men who find the love of their lives in the most unexpected place...enough suspense and drama that forms an incredible plot which will hold the reader spellbound from the start... Thanks go to Ms. Guillone for another amazing story. ~ *Fallen Angel Reviews*

Men of Phuket: Tongue-Thai'd is sweet enough to give you a cavity, and yet hot enough to scorch your tongue. Don't crack this book open without ice water! ~ *Author, Amanda Young*

Simmering and heartfelt. This endearing love story is sure to please. ~ *Author, Madelynne Ellis*

The love scenes between Nat and Ryu will leave you breathless...I know they did me. ~ *Author, Carol Lynne*

Total-E-Bound Publishing books in print from Sedonia Guillone:

Men of Tokyo: Sudden Bliss

Coming soon:

Fabulous Brits: Yin Yang
Men of Tokyo: Sudden Surrender

MEN OF PHUKET
TONGUE THAI'D

SEDONIA GUILLONE

MEN OF PHUKET

TONGUE THAI'D

Dedication

To Mitch. Without you, this book, title and all, wouldn't have come into being. I love you.

Thank You

As always, thanks to my critique partner, Ruth Axtell Morren for your input and honest feedback, to Claire for wanting me to be here at Total-E-Bound, and to Rawee and Vison Chong for showing me the beautiful book on Muay Thai that helped me write this book.

Author's Note

Here is a brief glossary of terms appearing in the book that might be unfamiliar:

Yakuza : Name for organised crime in Japan
Wakashu: literally "son" in the *yakuza* a man who is serving under his boss
Oyabun: the head of a crime family
-gumi: the suffix attached to the name of the family to denote the crime family as a whole. In this story, I refer to the Suzuki-gumi because their last name is Suzuki.

Yaoi: According to Wikipedia, "**Yaoi** (やおい) is a publishing genre which originated in Japan and often encompasses manga, dōjinshi, anime, and fan art. It is homosexual love between male characters and is sexually explicit."

Chapter One

Tokyo, Japan

"Ryu, come. It's time." Kiku held open the door, revealing the black sedan, windows tinted, idling in the back alley.

"This sucks." Ryu narrowed his eyes at the only man he'd ever loved. His hand tightened around the handles of his duffel bag.

Pain flashed across Kiku's dark eyes. "I know."

Ryu took a last look at his fellow White Tigers, his brothers on the path. They'd already said their goodbyes, but Ryu scanned their eyes. His gaze locked with Yuzo on the end.

Don't worry, Yuzo, I won't seduce your lover on the way to the airport. Ryu watched the thought rise in his mind and then let it pass. Pettiness was below a White Tiger, a trait completely lacking honour. As much as Ryu wanted to blame him, it wasn't Yuzo's fault that Kiku had fallen in love with him.

And it wasn't *really* Yuzo's fault that Ryu had to leave his home. Again.

He bowed to his brothers. "*Sayonara.*" There wasn't time to embrace them all a second time.

"Now, Ryu."

Ryu forced himself to turn and walk out. A guy in a dark suit and sunglasses opened the car door for him and Ryu had to remind himself he was being protected, not arrested. He felt like a criminal, stealing out in the still, humid air of dawn, rather than someone taking refuge *from* a criminal.

Kiku settled into the seat beside him and Ryu breathed a sigh of relief. At least he'd have this last car ride with him. The agent closed the door behind them, settled into the passenger seat and the driver started.

Ryu tried not to look through the dark tinting as Ni-Chome passed by him. At this hour, the bars and clubs lining their street were now closed, the neon signs dark, the sidewalks empty of the crowds who flocked Tokyo's hottest gay nightspots after sunset. He'd grown up in this neighbourhood. Twenty-seven years was a long time to be in one place. He sighed and looked down at his hand still gripping the handles of his duffel.

The car stopped at the intersection, a little too hard. The jarring motion almost threw him against Kiku. He clutched the hand rest in the door with his other hand, pulling himself in the opposite direction.

Not that it would matter. Kiku didn't love him *that* way. Life could really be cruel, making a person fall in love with someone who didn't fall in love with you back.

The car resumed and Ryu continued to stare down at his jeans.

"Ryu, please, look at me."

Ryu obeyed even though the other man's dark gaze captured his, as usual. There wasn't a time it hadn't, even when Ryu was thirteen and Kiku was a *wakashu*, coming to his house to bring Ryu's father his cut of the weekly earnings from his casino. Even then, Ryu had known Kikuchiya was different, not a true *yakuza*, not in his heart.

"I didn't have any choice. I pray you don't hate me."

Ryu stared at the face he'd always thought as beautiful as a golden Buddha, smooth skin, wide set eyes, high cheekbones and sensuous lips. *Hate him?* Hate the one man who'd cared about him, saw something special in him when no one gave a shit, not even his own mother? "I could never hate you. Ever."

Relief flitted through Kiku's features, though his look remained solemn. "This is one of the hardest things I've ever done."

Ryu's heart sped up a bit. "Really?"

The other man bowed his clean-shaven head. "Of course it is. Don't you understand? You're the best friend I've ever had."

Now his jaw nearly dropped. Ridiculous pleasure flushed through his chest. Could it possibly be true? Kiku was a man who expressed his emotions, but he'd never said anything like this, not even when they *were* lovers. "What about Yuzo?"

Kiku looked up. "Yuzo is sincere…I hope. He has stood by me through…this." Kiku held up his left hand. The second finger-cutting he'd been forced to commit to appease Taro Suzuki had finally healed over. "But you've stayed by me even though…" His gaze shifted towards the window.

The rest of the sentence they both knew.

"Don't make me go." Without thinking, Ryu grasped the other man's forearm. The muscle was hard under the thin sleeve of his shirt. "I'm older now. I box. I can face Suzuki. He won't ever be able to—"

"Don't say that word." Kiku's face darkened. "I won't let that psychopathic *yak* take you in trade for Yuzo and I *won't* ever let him touch you again. He's filth. You're...precious." His full lips pressed together and a muscle twitched in his jaw.

A memory flitted through Ryu's mind. *'Get the hell off him. He's a kid.'* Kiku had stalked into the dark bedroom and loomed over Suzuki and his goon. Suzuki had rolled right off Ryu and did up his pants. Everyone knew Kiku was fierce and one of Naboru Miyazaki's favourite 'sons'.

Suzuki had also been a *wakashu* at the time, a bitter one who resented being an underling with Kiku when his own father was the *oyabun* of the Suzuki-gumi. If the elderly man learned of this intended insult to Ryu's father, his chances of advancement would have completely vanished. However, that hadn't stopped Taro from making Kiku's life a constant hell, either. Which included his current demand for Ryu.

Ryu's hand still rested on Kiku's arm. Their gazes locked. Ryu kept his hand where it was. He never wanted to let go.

Through the car window, he caught a glance of the Sumida River as they crossed over. There was still a chunk of time left until they reached the airport, but the urgency Ryu felt only intensified.

He dared to inch closer.

Kiku didn't object. He reached up and fingered Ryu's spiky hair, as if testing the shocking pink dye. "You should cut these tips. You'll stand out."

Cut his hair? Hell no. "I'll be in *fucking* Thailand," he said using that popular English swear word he knew. "What difference does it make?" He didn't care that he sounded like the hoodlums he'd resisted becoming. "I want you to always be able to find me." He waited for Kiku to scold his language.

Instead, Kiku's touch slid down his cheek and he brushed one fingertip over the nose ring in Ryu's left nostril. "Not *fucking* Thailand, Ryu. *Phuket.*" Brief humour sparkled in Kiku's velvety eyes. "And I'll always come and find you if you need me." He tapped the nose ring. "This. Also too conspicuous."

Heat tingled in Ryu's cheeks. He'd never told Kiku his reason for getting the nose ring. No one knew. The others would tease him mercilessly for being a sap. At least, he believed they would. It didn't matter anyway. Kiku was psychic, practically a mind reader, and very likely had already guessed. Which was probably why he hadn't pushed Ryu to take it out before leaving.

Kiku's touch on his skin made his heartbeat rise. Without meaning to, he tilted his face upward. *Just one kiss*, he thought. Just to say good-bye.

Kiku's fingertips slid from his cheek. "It wouldn't be fair to you," he said softly.

Ryu's breath caught. "What wouldn't be fair?"

"What you were thinking."

Kuso! "Why don't you let *me* decide that? It seems to be the only thing I have any freaking control over in this situation."

The sorrow in Kiku's eyes shamed him. Kiku was the same man who'd taught him the path of the White Tiger, who'd showed him how to use sexual energy to heal his emotions. Just as sacred as their friendship was the relationship of teacher to student. He looked down. "I'm sorry," he murmured. "I shouldn't have spoken to you that—"

"Shh." Kiku's fingertips under his chin made him look up. Soft warm lips closed over his. Kiku's hand cupped his cheek again. Ryu's eyelids fluttered as he sank into the kiss. A thumb brushed his cheekbone, back and forth. Just like the first time Kiku had ever kissed him. Kiku's kiss. The one tender thing Ryu had ever experienced in his life, that showed him there was more to the world than *yakuza*, than organised crime and rape.

Ryu's arms and legs tingled. The gentle fire spread through his gut and made his dragon harden. He dared to let his hand wander under Kiku's loose fitting shirt and sweep his fingertips across one side of the other man's tight waist.

Kiku started slightly but remained in place, his hand caressing Ryu's cheek.

Ryu moaned through their kiss, uncaring about the men in the front seat who no doubt could hear every breath and sound. It had been so long since he'd felt Kiku's warm skin, the tight hard muscles underneath. So smooth and beautiful. He could imagine the white tigers inked onto Kiku's chest as his fingers passed over it, the tattoos that had once marked him as a *yakuza* but had come to symbolize his commitment to his faith.

The pad of his thumb brushed over Kiku's nipple. The larger man pulled in a tight breath and broke the kiss. "Ryu," he whispered, breathing heavily. His dark eyes had a hungry edge now and the skin of his face had darkened.

Ryu suppressed a grin. So, Kiku wasn't as immune to him as he came off. Just as soon, the shadow settled over his heart again. The message was clear. He pulled his hand out and rested it in his lap.

"It's my failing," Kiku said.

For a moment, the spike of hurt made Ryu want to agree. However, just looking into Kiku's eyes made his heart melt all over again. "It's no one's fault." His words were true, though he'd never stopped wishing things were like they'd been before Yuzo came along, when Kiku had shared his bed with him, taught him that sex could be beautiful, full of pleasure and not fear...

Kiku closed his hand over Ryu's and held it, resting their interlaced fingers on one hard thigh. Ryu sighed, grateful for the contact, which, to his relief, lasted the rest of the way to the airport.

Once there, Kiku accompanied him through the terminal building, flanked by plainclothes agents who made their little group appear more as a collection of friends come to see him off.

Ryu's heartbeat increased the closer they drew to the security checkpoint. At the small gate, he dropped his bag to the floor and threw his arms around Kiku. In a moment like this, he didn't give a shit about anything else, not even the tears that slipped from his eyes. Kiku and the others were going under heavy protection now. The Temple, their home and sanctuary would crawl with guards keeping an eye out for Suzuki and his goons. When the hell would he see Kiku again?

Thankfully, Kiku squeezed him back just as hard before pulling away. His dark eyes too, were misted over, as if he were holding back his emotions. "Don't neglect your meditation," he said softly, "partner or no partner."

Ryu swallowed hard. "I won't. But I'm coming back to you when this is over."

To his surprise, a tiny smile teased the corners of Kiku's lips. "I hope you won't want to."

Ryu stared at him. The words spiralled strangely through him and if Kiku hadn't been so damn weirdly psychic, he wouldn't have thought much of them. But before he could ask Kiku what he'd meant, the agent pressed the handle of his bag into his hand and steered him towards security.

* * * *

Bangkok, Thailand

Ryu Miyazaki, age twenty-seven, height: five-foot-seven inches, mother Mali Miyazaki, native of Bangkok, Thailand, Father, Naboru Miyazaki…

Nat re-read that last line, still disbelieving. Naboru Miyazaki, the WBA welterweight champion? Sure, it had been almost three decades since the boxer's illustrious career had ended, but one fighter never forgot a predecessor. He shook his head. What made a professional athlete turn to crime? According to the notes before him, Miyazaki was pretty high up in the Suzuki-gumi, by reputation one of Tokyo's fiercest and most prevalent crime families. True, winning most of your fights didn't guarantee an easy ride afterward. Life still went on. If anyone knew that, Nat did. But the *yakuza*? No good.

He sighed and looked again at the photo of Miyazaki's son, included in the faxed over materials. Nat could definitely see the guy's resemblance to his father, well, except for the hot pink spiky hair and nose ring.

"Don't you get sick reading in a car, Phoenix?"

Nat looked up.

Agent Tongmee chuckled. "Just wondering." There was an amusement in the younger man's eyes that made an uncomfortable heat in Nat's cheeks, as if he'd been staring a drop too long at the photograph. Nat sensed a hint of resentment. Tongmee hadn't been thrilled about being taken off the human trafficking detail in Bangkok to do what he considered babysitting the brat offspring of a *yakuza*, especially one who was coming to them from what appeared a gay men's hotel, or something like that. Tongmee's brother had been gay and died recently of AIDS, and Tongmee, still bitter, hadn't grasped the notion that you didn't need to hate an entire population of people who weren't at fault for such a tragedy. Unfortunately for Tongmee, he was one of the only agents in the Naresuan 261 fluent in Japanese.

Nat closed the dossier and glanced out the window. They were on the Phahon Yothan road now and he could see Don Muang Airport in the near distance. The hot tropical sun flashed off its modern glass towers. He shifted slightly in his seat. No wonder Tongmee had remarked. How long had he been absorbed in studying the file?

"Remind me again why a counter-terrorism unit of five men is needed to protect this brat?"

Nat suppressed a sigh. Briefly he wondered if there was some bad karma he'd earned to end up with Tongmee in his command. "I wasn't told everything." Tongmee knew that. Why make him go over it again? "The son of the main boss has threatened him and a diplomat in Tokyo arranged all this to protect him."

Tongmee made a scoffing sound. "Whatever they say."

Nat looked at him then back out the window. Tongmee didn't need to know that Ryu Miyazaki had refused to take a fall for Suzuki in a fight. However, the situation from there got murky. Why send him to Thailand? And how was it that a Japanese diplomat went to all this trouble to protect Miyazaki, mobilizing any number of agents and going to the cost of transporting him here to be protected by the same agents used to guard the Thai royals and foreign ambassadors when they travelled in Thailand? There were too many questions here, but Nat wasn't in a place to demand answers. His job was to protect the guy. So that's what he was going to do.

The driver turned onto the perimeter road of the airport, following the signs that led to the international flight concourses. Minutes later, the Air Japan sign was visible and the car pulled up to the curb. Nat slipped the folder into his duffel bag. He got out and scanned the sidewalk. Agent Chuek, dressed in a baggy T-shirt and jeans, was up ahead, and Agents Seinalloy and Pettoh, similarly dressed, were already inside the concourse, probably heading towards the customs exit where they'd melt into the background of the busy modern, window-encased building.

Tongmee fell into step beside him as they entered the glass building. He too, would never be tagged as a government agent in his button-down baggy shirt, Thai fisherman pants and sandals. "Hope he's gotten rid of the electric hair," he said. "Otherwise, he'll stand out like the wreath on Chulalongkorn Day."

Nat ignored the quip and pulled off his sunglasses, folding them as he and Tongmee followed the signs towards customs. Miyazaki's plane was landing now and he'd be out before long. "He's going into hiding," he answered finally, not breaking his stride. "No doubt he'll have dyed or cut it and taken out the nose ring."

"You'd hope." Tongmee chuckled and again the sound gave Nat a weird feeling, as if Tongmee had caught him considering Miyazaki longer than was necessary.

They drew closer to the customs exit just as Miyazaki's Air Japan flight was announced. Nat stood off to the side with Tongmee, watching the passengers file out of customs. So far, several young men in Miyazaki's age group had come through, but none of them was him. From the photo, the guy had a surprisingly guileless look, one Nat wouldn't have expected from the son of a *yakuza* boss. Maybe that's why Nat had stared a bit too long at the photo, wondering how

Miyazaki could have possibly held onto a look of innocence. Yeah, innocence was the word, in spite of the—

Pink spiky hair.

The splash of colour struck Nat's gaze. Not just pink. Nat stared as Miyazaki—no doubt this was him—emerged from customs, a small gym bag slung over one shoulder, accompanied by a second man. Hot, shocking, pink.

Miyazaki drew closer and Nat saw the glint of gold around his left nostril. Was this truly possible? Did the kid even have half a brain in his head? Tongmee's joke about the floral wreath came to mind. In spite of the fact that his fellow agent was obnoxious and bitter, he'd been right. A dead man could pick Miyazaki from a crowd.

The hair and nose ring had to go. As soon as possible.

Nat felt an elbow nudge his ribs. He glanced sideways at Tongmee, not returning the grin. "Come on," he said.

A more normal-looking agent, the one who'd no doubt accompanied Miyazaki on the flight, walked beside him, dressed in casual shirt and jeans. Miyazaki would have looked normal too in his long-sleeve black button down shirt, hip-level jeans and boots. But he didn't.

Working to keep his demeanour calm, Nat signalled to the agent who noticed him immediately and guided his charge in their direction.

As Miyazaki drew closer, Nat noticed that innocent expression of his looked distinctly sullen. No mystery there. Being forced into hiding wasn't exactly conducive to peace and happiness.

Another moment and they were face to face. Up close, the electric pink hair was quite distracting, the only thing that pulled Nat's gaze away from Miyazaki's almond-shaped eyes and the woodsy scent he emitted, like incense burning on a temple altar. "Welcome to Thailand," Nat began, "I'm—"

Miyazaki's eyes widened. "I know who you are. Nat Phoenix. I'm honoured." His voice had a hushed sound of wonder.

"Thank you." Nat tried to ignore the flush of warmth in his chest. It had been a long time since he'd met someone who knew him anymore.

Miyazaki bowed. When he straightened, that guileless tinge in his dark eyes had returned and he was staring at Nat in a way that made him seem oblivious to the entire world, including Tongmee.

Nat returned the bow, then stared at him. "You speak Thai." Perfectly, in fact, from what he just heard. He glanced quickly at Tongmee who now wore an expression that said, 'Great, you didn't need me here after all.'

Miyazaki nodded. "My mother is Thai. She refuses to speak Japanese." His gaze darted to Tongmee and back, as if he'd just become aware of the surrounding world again.

"This is Tongmee," Nat said, omitting the title of 'Agent' before his partner's name. He couldn't take any risk of being overheard. "Now, we're going to the restroom."

"All right."

Nat called Pettoh on his cell phone and explained where they were headed. The immediate need was to get Miyazaki's electric pink head covered. He turned to Tongmee. "Go to a gift shop and get a hat, a baseball cap will do, and meet me in the men's room." Tongmee nodded and took off.

"What's going on?" Miyazaki asked.

"Come with me." He ushered the smaller man through the doorless entry of the men's room. The place was huge with probably thirty stalls in addition to the urinals, but Nat steered Miyazaki towards the back, which wasn't crowded at all. He pushed open a door. "Go in there."

"What?"

"You heard me, get in." He stepped forward, using his own broad frame and greater height to herd Miyazaki backward, then crowded into the stall with him and shut the door, sliding the lock into place.

"What the—"

"Shh." Nat put his finger to his lips. Around them, the sounds of doors opening and closing, toilets flushing and men pissing into urinals and using the sinks muffled their voices. Still, you could never be too cautious. "You have to cover your hair," he said softly so as not to be heard over the other sounds.

Miyazaki's eyes widened with a look of panic. "No. I can't do that."

Nat suppressed a flash of anger. Maybe Tongmee was right after all. Maybe this guy was just a brat. "You can and you will."

A strange look passed across Miyazaki's face. He crossed his arms in front of him. "No, I won't."

Nat put his hands flat on the walls on either side of the stall and leaned in closer. Miyazaki's woodsy aroma floated to his nostrils. Nat had several inches in height over the guy and had to bow his head to make eye contact. "Look, I don't know how it is with the cops in Japan, but in Thailand, you'll be treated well only as long as you're cooperative."

"I'm not trying to be uncooperative. You...don't *understand*." The look of panic remained in his eyes.

Was this kid for real? Or was that greeting he'd given moments before a way of trying to control Nat through flattery? It sure as hell wasn't going to work. "Then make me understand."

Miyazaki's arms went to his sides. He glanced away then bowed his head. "I can't."

Nat found himself staring at the hot pink tips of hair. Hard to believe this guy was twenty-seven years old. "Then have a seat. Make yourself comfortable until Tongmee gets back. With your *hat*."

Obediently, Miyazaki lowered himself onto the toilet seat, hands folded in his lap like a good little schoolboy.

Miyazaki was weird. Nat knew from his dossier that he practiced some strange religion, an offshoot of Taoism. He didn't know the details, but whatever it was had rendered the man weird. Weird, but...strangely beautiful.

Nat found himself staring down at him, the way he had at the photograph. The grainy faxed picture hadn't done Miyazaki justice. He was a less rugged, much better looking version of his father. Softly rounded features, cheekbones, chin, nose, lips, and really long lashes, barely any beard or moustache, all like the image of a classically beautiful man in a Japanese woodblock print a fan in Tokyo had gifted Nat after his championship fight so long ago. The only thing Thai about him was the darker golden hue of his skin. With the exception of a few nicks on brow and cheekbones obviously gotten from boxing matches, his face was perfection.

Nat's gaze strayed again to Miyazaki's lips, shaped in a way that made him appear permanently as if he were waiting to be kissed...

Shit. *Not* going there. Nat pretended his groin hadn't just tightened a notch. Beautiful or not, Miyazaki hadn't been in his care five minutes and was already being difficult. Nat did not entertain the possibility of sex with the son of a *yakuza* boss who, like his father, believed he was somehow outside the bounds of the law.

Suddenly, Miyazaki lifted his gaze to Nat's.

Nat returned the look, expecting Miyazaki to look away but he didn't.

His deep-set eyes seemed to scan Nat with an evaluating air. "I'm not what you think I am," he said softly.

Nat couldn't quite distinguish the tone of the statement. More self-defence than anything else from what he could surmise. "And what do I think you are?" The question was out before he realised what he was doing.

"An amoral brat."

Nat's heart jumped. Was this kid a mind reader or something? "What makes you think that's my opinion of you?"

Miyazaki shrugged. The sullen, somewhat mournful look had returned to his beautiful face. "I just sensed that's what you were thinking. But it's not true."

Nat cleared his throat. "Is that so?"

"Yes. That's so."

"Well, then prove me wrong."

Ryu sighed. To think he'd fantasised a million times about sucking this guy's dragon!

Had Kiku known that Nat Phoenix was to be the agent in charge when he and the Tokyo police inspector with the diplomat father had arranged all this? Couldn't be. Kiku would never release one of his White Tigers into the care of some inhuman brute, especially Ryu. Ryu was used to being threatened by *yakuza*, freaking amoral thugs. Not by a world champion boxer whose techniques, skill and well, physical hotness he'd admired for more than ten years.

Shimatta! He was trembling now, felt the heat of sweat erupt in his armpits. Phoenix was bigger and stronger than he was, and even though Ryu knew how to fight, he didn't have a chance against a guy this size, especially one with Phoenix's skill and speed.

His pulses throbbed in his own ears. If he *really* needed to defend himself, he could use the nerve press Kiku had shown him long ago, shortly after the rape. But that was only for the most desperate self-defence, when your very life was threatened. Press too hard in the right places and bam…the guy would be dead. And even then, you had to be in just the correct position to hit the nerves that mattered.

Phoenix still stood with his palms pressed to either side of the cubicle, gaze trained just over Ryu's head, as if he were studying the wall behind him. He shifted suddenly and leaned back against the door, arms folded in front of him. Every corded muscle in his arms flexed with movement, which caused his white T-shirt to stretch more tightly over his broad chest.

A shudder of energy travelled through Ryu's body. Heat tingled in his nipples and down in his dragon, which started to get hard. However, his mind was muddled, making him unclear as to whether his sexual response was from attraction or from fear.

That's when he felt it. Phoenix's energy. The man's yang force filled the cubicle like a wild beast's. Ryu could practically smell the testosterone in the air. He thought of the way Phoenix had been staring at him a few moments before, as if he were hungry and Ryu was a nice plate of sushi. How many guests at the White Tiger had stared at him that way? Plenty. And the ones who looked at him that way never made it past Kiku's psychic evaluation. Kiku never left Ryu alone with anyone whom he felt wasn't completely gentle.

But Kiku wasn't here.

A lump formed in Ryu's throat, threatening to choke off his air. What if Phoenix tried to hurt him? The man could overpower him easily, especially in this tiny space. Ryu felt his trapped state the way a caged tiger must feel. He was completely in this man's power. Whatever Phoenix wanted to do with him, he could. And even if Ryu managed to get away from him somehow, he was in a strange land with no friends. His mother's relatives lived somewhere in Bangkok but he wouldn't begin to know how to find them. His only advantage was he spoke the language...

Ryu's breath tightened and his heartbeat sped up. He felt like he had when he was seventeen, the night he opened his eyes and found Suzuki and his goon hovering over his bed in the middle of the night...

"Are you all right?"

Ryu tensed. Only then did he realise the position he was in that had inspired Phoenix's question. Both hands clutched into his hair, forehead against his palms, elbows on his knees, breath nearly gasping. He slipped his hands away and straightened. "I'm fine."

Phoenix was looking down at him, only this time, his expression had lost its hunger. He nodded, though he appeared doubtful.

Ryu cleared his throat and returned the look, determined not to appear frightened. This seemed a good chance to study Phoenix's face for any signs of compassion, the kind he saw in Kiku's face all those years ago that had given him hope.

Phoenix was ten years older than Ryu, yet he looked just as formidable as he had in his boxing days. He still wore his thick ebony hair the way he had then, very short around the sides, long enough on top to form shiny waves. His face was a rugged map of his fights, nicks and scars here and there, interrupting the burnt-toffee hue of his skin, toughening the appearance of his high, sharp cheekbones and angular jaw.

Ryu looked into the man's eyes, which were very large and nearly round like a Westerner's eyes under thick fringes of ebony lashes. Zeroing in on the chocolate-coloured irises,

Ryu studied them, as if his life depended on making the right judgment call. To his relief, the anger that had flashed through Phoenix's eyes earlier wasn't there. Ryu peered closer, nearly pulling in a breath. Could he possibly be seeing clearly? Did he see—

"Phoenix?"

Phoenix unfolded his arms and turned around. "Down here."

In the next second a black baseball cap appeared over the top of the stall door. "Thanks, Tongmee." Phoenix took it and turned around, holding the cap out. "Put this on if you want to leave the bathroom today."

Ryu winced, as much at the statement as at the cap. He'd had his chance to explain why he couldn't cover his hair, couldn't make himself less visible in case Kiku had to come find him. But then he'd known a guy like Phoenix would have called him a baby and told him he was being stupid. That much was obvious from the man's brutish behaviour so far. And he'd had enough in his life of having his privates, both physical and emotional, exposed to cruel men. Screw Phoenix. Well, not literally. No matter how good-looking he was.

The cap hung from Phoenix's wide, strong-looking fingers. "Well?" he said. "Today?"

Ryu took the cap. He looked down at it, fighting back the sense of panic engulfing him. He needed to appear calm no matter what. Phoenix would just call him a baby otherwise and use his weakness against him.

"You can put it on backwards if you want. If you think it looks better."

To Ryu's surprise, Phoenix's tone was almost conciliatory, as if he'd decided to drop the sarcasm.

"Look, we still have another flight to catch. That gives us just enough time to get to the right concourse and grab a bite to eat. You must be hungry."

Ryu couldn't even *think* of food, his stomach was so tight. But Phoenix sounded as if he were trying to be nice and Ryu's training kicked in. A White Tiger always responded to courtesy with courtesy. He slipped the cap on, backwards as suggested, even though his heart was pounding again.

"Thank you." Phoenix's expression was unreadable, but at least his demeanour was calm again, businesslike. He slid the lock and held open the stall door.

With a glance, Ryu brushed past him. A trace of Phoenix's yang energy radiated around the man, a stark reminder of the power coiled within that physique. If Ryu thought the open stall door meant freedom, the truth was painfully clear. The other agent, the guy called Tongmee stood there, watching him emerge, an amused look in his eyes.

The urge to glare at him rose, but Ryu squelched it. Tongmee was shorter and slimmer than Phoenix but the energy he radiated felt more brutish. Another guy who could overpower him and probably outrun him.

Ryu sighed and walked between them, out of the men's room. For someone who was being protected, he felt more like a prisoner than anything else. He kept his gaze on the floor just ahead of each step he took, vividly aware of his powerlessness. He'd almost always felt this way, with only brief periods of relief while learning the White Tiger path. Now, an old feeling resurged, one he'd thought had been healed under Kiku's care and caresses. He hadn't experienced it since childhood when it had been intense, especially during the aftermath of what Suzuki had done to him.

Hopelessness. Deep and painful. With no chance of escape.

Chapter Two

"Is this your first time in Thailand?" Nat tried to engage Miyazaki in a bit of conversation. If the guy had seemed morose after getting off the plane from Japan, his mood had progressively darkened since leaving the men's room.

Miyazaki had remained silent during their brief meal in an airport sushi bar and had proven equally as taciturn during the shuttle flight to Phuket. Something about wearing the hat seemed to distress him to no end. Nat would have dismissed it as vanity but Miyazaki didn't strike him as particularly superficial, especially after that near panic attack in the bathroom stall, the way he'd been shaking and looked up at Nat as if Nat were a rampaging elephant about to flatten him...

Miyazaki looked at him, seeming surprised by the attempt to make small talk. "Yes. I've...never been out of Tokyo. Not unless you count Yokohama. That's about twenty minutes' drive away."

A surprisingly long answer to his question. Nat sat up a bit straighter, aware of the disdainful look Miyazaki had just received from Tongmee who sat on his other side in the car. Nat glanced at Seinalloy who drove and repressed the urge to scold the other agent. Tongmee would really need to behave himself, no matter how grief-stricken he was. "Yokohama, is that another city?" Best to keep the conversation going if he could.

Miyazaki nodded. His soft features brightened a bit. "Kiku's mother lives there. I've gone with him to visit her."

Kikuchiya Fujimara. The name was in the dossier. Apparently, he was some sort of religious leader...or something. A former *yakuza* who'd gone straight, according to the notes. His exact relationship to Miyazaki on paper was unclear, though the tone of Miyazaki's voice when he mentioned Fujimara was obviously one of deep affection. Maybe more.

Suddenly, Miyazaki looked down. He fell silent as if worried about giving away a secret.

Nat sighed and glanced out the window, at the familiar stretch of palm tree-lined beach the car followed towards Phuket City. He fought the urge to close his eyes against the ghosts this place dredged up. The life he'd left behind so long ago. Even knowing the images were really memories in his mind didn't make them any less real. Him and Aran racing along the sand, wrestling, laughing, sparring...

"I saw your last fight."

The soft voice pulled Nat's gaze from the window, out of his memories.

Miyazaki was looking at him. A shy look tinged his eyes and Nat sensed he was trying to return the attempt at conversation.

Nat blinked. "I'm sorry?"

"I saw your last fight. Back in two-thousand. In Tokyo. Against Nidokki."

The admiration had returned to Miyazaki's tone, making Nat remember his fight against the Japanese boxer defending his championship title. Though in the same weight category, Nidokki had been taller and heavier, and the world didn't really believe Nat Phoenix had a great chance to beat him.

"That was the best fight I've ever seen."

Again, that flush of warmth spread through Nat's chest. Even though he'd won, that fight had cost him physically, enough that he'd decided to retire and not risk worse injuries in defending the title. "Thank you." He tried to discern any manipulation in Miyazaki but couldn't. The guy seemed sincere enough.

On the other side, Tongmee coughed then fell silent. Miyazaki glanced at him then down at his hands, giving Nat the distinct sense the other agent made him uncomfortable. Briefly he wished Tongmee had ridden in the second car with Chuek and Pettoh.

Nat cast about for something else to say. He didn't want to question Miyazaki about his own truncated boxing career. No doubt that would be a sore topic, nor did he want to bring up the White Tiger place he came from in front of Tongmee. Finally, he found a safe topic. "Have you ever watched Muay Thai?"

Miyazaki shook his head. "Only a little bit. Where I trained, there were some guys who practiced it." He cleared his throat, looking suddenly shy. "I know that you began with it."

The bit of colour darkening his cheeks told Nat that Miyazaki had followed his career. He wondered how much.

"If I may ask, why didn't you go on to teach it? I bet a million students would come to you."

Nat looked down. His reason really was very personal, too personal to share with someone he'd just met. When he looked up, Miyazaki's gaze was resting on him.

A light passed through the other man's eyes, as if he'd understood. "I guess you wanted a change," he said softly.

Nat stared at him briefly, too stunned for a moment at Miyazaki's sensitivity. If that's what it was. "Yes," he answered after a few seconds. "I did need a change." That much had been true.

"Agent Phoenix?" Miyazaki looked puzzled and again, alarm showed in his eyes. The way he was acting gave Nat the impression he felt like a powerless being, carted around at others' wills.

"You can call me Nat." Maybe that would make him a little more comfortable.

Miyazaki blinked and gave a brief nod, as if using his first name were not something he could do. The alarm didn't leave his eyes. "Where are we going?"

"I'm taking you to Suwat training camp. It's where I started." Nat looked out the window again, glancing at the beachside resort town, at the colourful signs, endless cafés and souvenir shops cluttering the sidewalks. Not to mention the sea of beachgoers everywhere enjoying Phuket's laid back, anything goes atmosphere. "I'm sorry. I needed to tell you that earlier." Had he really been so absorbed in looking at Miyazaki he'd forgotten to do his job properly? He'd have to be more careful.

"Training camp?"

Nat suppressed a sigh of frustration. Why did Miyazaki have to sound so alarmed at everything? "Yes. I'll explain everything as soon as we get there."

Miyazaki fell silent and sat back. His soft lips were pursed as if he had something to say and was deciding the better of it in the interest of keeping peace.

Seinalloy made a turn onto Choa Fa Road and Nat's stomach gave a small flip. In mere minutes they'd be at the training camp. For a moment, his mind blurred, making him uncertain as to why he would have chosen this place to hide Miyazaki. There were a million training camps all over Thailand, every single one of which would welcome Nat Phoenix's presence. Why come back here, so close to the pain?

He sighed. Phuket had been the best location he could think of. The *yakuza* who came to Thailand to traffic stayed in Bangkok with easier access to hub ports and airports. The chances of running into trouble here were less. Plus, with the vibrant gay community, maybe the guy had a better chance of blending in. He sure as hell wouldn't blend too well in the countryside. In dress, and manner, even without the pink hair and nose ring, no one would take Ryu Miyazaki for the son of a local rice farmer, or something equally as humble.

Seinalloy turned at the sign for the gym and stopped in the small dirt parking area. The late afternoon sun slanted off the metal roof and a light breeze rustled the leaves of the palm trees flanking the gym. Nat sighed and took up the handles of his bag. "This is it." Without looking at his charge's expression, he got out. When Tongmee had Miyazaki between the two of them, Nat led the way. The sooner they got into their room, the sooner he could go back to work on getting rid of the guy's hot pink hair and nose ring.

"The great Nat Phoenix!"

They 'd only gone twenty feet into the long open corrugated metal building when Lew came towards them.

Nat smiled at the paunchy little man who'd known him when Aran was still alive and had let the two of them hang around and use the equipment even though they didn't have money for training. He bowed to his old friend. "Thank you, Lew."

Lew returned the bow, all smiles. "You're here with your new student. Thank Buddha." The older man bowed to Miyazaki then looked back to Nat. "I've been so anxious to see you since you called to say you're coming back. My joy is very great. And to know that you have finally decided to train someone." His large dark eyes looked misted. "So many people will be so happy."

Nat's heart thudded a bit. Even in his heyday, he'd never been completely comfortable with adoration. Aran was the one who would have loved it and who would have been champion first. "Thank you." He gave a brief introduction and then asked to settle into the room. A nod to Tongmee sent him to situate the other agents and then make a round of the entire place before stationing himself outside Nat and Miyazaki's room.

Lew bowed again. "Of course. Of course." He waddled forward on what was an injured leg from a run in with an elephant long ago. "You'll stay as long as you want, no charge. And you take an air-conditioned room."

"Thank you, Lew." He didn't argue with his old friend, but knew he'd somehow manage to get the money to him. Crowded into the small space with Miyazaki, they would need the air to be cooler. Tongmee and the others had a room in the nearby guesthouse where Lew sent training camp guests who spilled over from his small place. "If you have an extra cot?"

Lew nodded. "Of course. I'll get that for you." He led them past the boxing ring on its platform surrounded by all the training equipment. At the very end of the corridor, he pushed open a guest room door. "This one will be the quietest, although you can see, not so quiet." He motioned towards the boxing ring where two young guys were sparring under the direction of one of the camp's trainers. They were engrossed and didn't seem to notice anyone coming in. Just as well, Nat thought. He didn't have a good feeling about the next hour or so of trying to get Miyazaki's pink hair cut off. Best to do it now, though, when he might be tired from a whole day of travelling.

"Not a problem, Lew."

"Here you go." Lew rushed into the tiny room ahead of them and put on the window rattler. The compressor hummed loudly, drowning out the noises from the gym. "I hope you'll be comfortable. I put in clean towels and extra bedding. Here's the TV, clothing rack and shelves for your things. When you're settled I'll introduce you to everyone. They're so excited."

Nat nodded. "Perfect. Thank you." From the corner of his eye, he watched Miyazaki take in his new accommodations, his bag hanging from one hand. The tiny square room barely had enough space to hold the double bed, small iron clothing rack and TV stand with a couple of shelves underneath it for storage. Miyazaki's eyes widened at the tiny bathroom. Guess he wasn't used to having a shower stall with a toilet in it. With his background, he was probably accustomed to luxurious living conditions.

Lew bowed again. "I'll let you get comfortable. If you need anything, just call. I'm in my office. Anytime, day or night. I'll leave the cot outside your door if you're busy."

Nat bowed to his old friend. "Thank you. I'm…glad to be back."

When Lew had gone, Nat turned to his charge. Miyazaki had pulled off the hat and set his bag on the floor and stood, quietly, watching Nat in a way that made him wonder whether he had purposely mastered the whipped dog expression he was wearing.

"I'm sorry about the conditions," Nat said. "I know they're a bit...crude."

Miyazaki shrugged, dropping the hat onto the bed. "They're okay." He sighed and his almond-shaped brown eyes took another once–over of the room. He remained where he was, giving Nat the impression he was afraid to move.

Nat sighed. "Look, I'm sorry we have to be crowded in together." Why he felt suddenly so apologetic, he didn't know. He was just trying to do his job. "I'm going to have a cot. The bed is all yours."

The guy nodded, still with a beaten expression. "As long as no one hurts me, I'm fine with whatever."

A strange shiver passed through Nat's chest and down his arms. Was Miyazaki referring to him? "No one's going to hurt you. I'm trying to help you. Maybe you don't understand that."

Miyazaki looked down, as if he were studying his boots. Head to toes the guy was an image from a fashion magazine, and it was hard to picture him dancing around in a boxing ring, landing punches and taking them. "I understand protection."

Nat's heartbeat sped up slightly. "Good, because that is precisely why I'm going to ask you to let me cut your hair."

Miyazaki's eyes went wide. That damnable look of panic flooded his soft features. "No. I told you, I can't."

"The nose ring too has to go." Nat steeled himself against Miyazaki's expression. Whether the guy was being manipulative or not didn't matter. Bottom line was he was acting stupidly and against his best interest. "You stick out like a sore thumb." He took a step closer and saw Miyazaki wince. "You can't rely on a hat. Especially if you're going to be training. It could fall off. You need to blend in a bit."

"No."

Nat suppressed a flash of anger. "Yes. Or you won't leave this room. You can stay holed up in here until I hear from Tokyo that you're free to leave."

"That's fine with me. I don't want to go anywhere."

Nat crossed his arms. "Giving me an attitude won't help you. In case you haven't learned that."

Alarm passed over Miyazaki's face. "I'm not trying to give you an attitude. I swear." He glanced away and then back. "It won't matter about my hair anyway. I have…tattoos. You can't cut *them* out."

"Tattoos can be covered." He gestured towards Miyazaki. "I don't see any on you now."

"Under these clothes, maybe." Miyazaki's hands went to the buttons of his shirt. "But I can't wear jeans in the ring."

Tingles ran down Nat's arms. "What are you doing?"

"Showing you what I mean." Miyazaki's fingers worked open his black shirt and the material fell to each side. With a quick yank, he slid the shirt off.

Nat stared. *Loog ga ree.* Son of a bitch. 'Tattoos' was an understatement. Miyazaki's whole torso was a canvas of colour and design. For a moment, Nat's mind blurred. All he could see were swirling patterns of leaping white tigers across Miyazaki's chest, ribcage and abdomen. Nat pulled in a breath. Heat erupted in his armpits.

Miyazaki stood, watching him, his arms at his sides. The rounded muscles of his shoulders too, were inked, the colours reaching to his carved-looking triceps. "See?"

Nat swallowed hard. He hadn't meant to notice the v-shape of the other man's torso or the lean perfection of his wiry musculature. If it hadn't been for his soft facial expressions, Miyazaki would have been the picture of a tough fighter. He was small, a welterweight, but like his face, his upper body was perfect.

Nat cleared his throat. The lubrication needed to speak seemed to have dried up in the last few seconds. "You can wear a shirt when you go outside," he managed to say. "No big deal."

Miyazaki didn't answer. Instead, he began toeing off his boots then undid the button and zipper of his jeans.

More electric heat zinged through Nat's body. What the hell was this guy doing?

Before he could even turn around, Miyazaki had shucked off his jeans and straightened again. "It won't work." He pointed down.

Nat wanted to close his eyes. But he couldn't. The bottom half of Miyazaki was as colourful…and…perfect as the top half. And well, he could see just about all of it. Including the hints of dark hair just above his…package, barely concealed by a pouch of white cloth. The rest of his underwear was a couple of strings across his hips and…Miyazaki turned around…up the crack of his ass, both cheeks of which were covered in colourful swirling designs. Purples, blues, reds, oranges and yellows…

To Nat's horror, his mouth began to water, as if the colours inked onto Miyazaki's smooth skin were flavours he could lick right off.

"I told you," Miyazaki said. He sounded a bit petulant, though the tone of his soft voice had dropped a notch.

From about mid-thigh to just below his collarbone, he was covered, a literal human canvas. Nat's gaze travelled over the perfect round globes of his ass, up his widening back where two *samurai* warriors in flowing kimonos fanned out, arms entwined, lips pressed together in a tender kiss.

Nat began to pace in the small room, the only way he could think of to relieve the sudden pressure in his groin. It occurred to him that Miyazaki could just be playing a game, using seduction to control him when flattery hadn't worked. "It's not going to work you know."

"What's not going to work?"

Nat glanced up. Miyazaki had turned back around to face him. His wide-eyed gaze almost made Nat think he really didn't know. "The seduction thing. Getting undressed like that." He gestured. "No matter what you do, I'm not going to let you keep that electric hair so that everyone will remember you at first glance. That's a good way to get *killed*."

Miyazaki's soft lips parted and his eyes grew even wider. "I wasn't trying to...seduce you." He looked down and Nat could swear he saw the other man's cheeks flush a shade darker.

Then something else occurred to him. "You *are* a *yakuza*, aren't you?"

At that, Miyazaki whipped his head up, eyes pained, as if he'd been physically slapped. "I am not a yak."

Nat crossed his arms, pinning Miyazaki with his gaze. "Then why are you marked up like one?" The thought that the guy was a criminal helped take the edge off Nat's physical response to his incredible, nearly-naked physique.

For a moment, Miyazaki's eyes misted over, as if he would burst into tears. But he remained silent and then squared his shoulders, causing the white tigers across his front to shift. "That's personal."

Nat uncrossed his arms and took a step towards Miyazaki. "Don't you ever just answer a question? How the hell am I supposed to help you if you won't tell me what I need to know?"

Again, silence. And that soft yet somewhat defiant look.

Dammit. He exhaled and turned his back to Miyazaki. "Why don't you...I don't know...get dressed, or shower or something. Not that it matters. You're not going out of this room anyway."

"I'd like to shower."

"Fine." He heard sounds of Miyazaki rummaging in his bag, probably for a toiletry kit or something followed by the door to the tiny bathroom closing and the spray of the shower.

Finally Nat turned around. Miyazaki's clothing was off the floor and neatly folded on the foot of the bed. Nat looked at the closed door. That's when the idea hit him. Quickly he formulated his plan to deal with Miyazaki's hair, then got ready. First to change into something looser and more comfortable. He opted for no shirt and a pair of fisherman pants. Then he called Lew's office to ask to borrow a pair of electric hair clippers — Lew always had one of those around — then called Tongmee to come to the room to help him.

The hot water felt good. Almost good enough to wash away how shitty he felt.

Ryu closed his eyes and let the spray douse his hair. He rubbed the bar of soap into the wet washcloth only to find his hands still shook. The soap slipped to the floor and skidded to the base of the toilet.

"*Shimatta.*" He crouched to retrieve it and wrapped it in the washcloth to use it that way. Soon, the sandalwood fragrance of the soap diffused over his skin and made a bit of tension run from his body. Phoenix's accusation still rang in his ears.

Seduction. He *hadn't* been trying to do that when he'd stripped down to his g-string.

Had he?

Ryu rubbed the soap and cloth over his chest. Tension still coiled in his limbs and down in his groin. His dragon was half-hard, hanging with a kind of insistent pressure. He sighed at the overabundance of yang that had built up inside him. He needed release, especially after all the turmoil. It had been wrong to go too long without a proper partner. Kiku had offered so many times to match him up with someone so that the yang force he cultivated from the guests he cared for would get channelled in a constructive way. Kiku was good at matching partners, too. Koji and Naoto were madly in love and both had reached Heaven together through the practices.

But then, neither Naoto nor Koji had the history with Kiku that he had. It was easy for them to be with each other and not wish all the time that they were with Kiku instead. Kiku hadn't been their first real lover and they hadn't shared his bed for years only to have him fall in love with someone else…

Ryu made a sound of frustration. Now he was stuck in this tiny room with Mega Cop. A bully on the right side of the law. What was the damn difference? He glanced down at his dragon, almost completely hard in spite of everything. Well, he often got aroused when afraid. And Mega Cop sure as shit made him feel afraid. As if everything else wasn't going wrong, one of his heroes had turned out to be a real jerk off.

A quick look at the door gave him a bit of relief. Some privacy, a few minutes to himself where Mega Cop couldn't control him.

Closing his eyes, he leaned back against the tiled wall, letting the spray batter his skin with soothing heat. Best thing was to tap off the excess yang. Perhaps then he'd think more clearly and be able to distinguish between fear and arousal. He palmed the length of his dragon and rubbed. Slowly at first, in controlled strokes, until his breathing and his hand moved together.

Damn, that felt better than the hot water. The contact of his hand against his cock made heat tingle along the shaft, causing pleasant waves that radiated into his yang sac. With his other hand, he squeezed his pearls, letting one finger dip down towards his hole. He shut his eyes and focused his attention. The rest of the world faded. His mind relaxed, cleared, like a calm lake before sunrise.

Unbidden, his age-old fantasy came to mind. He tried to push the image away, tried not to imagine himself on his knees in front of Nat Phoenix, tasting that delicious cock while his hands caressed Phoenix's smooth hips and rock hard ass. He opened his eyes but nothing would dispel the image. The desire in his body had taken over, erasing Phoenix's toughness, dictating the direction of Ryu's thoughts.

Giving in, Ryu let himself fantasise. He closed his eyes again as he stroked himself, imagining the taste and feel of Phoenix's dragon against his tongue, the fullness of it in his mouth, the sound of Phoenix's groans or how he might clutch Ryu's hair and pump his hips in a rhythm against the sucking.

Stifling a moan of pleasure, he increased the rhythm. Squeeze, stroke. Squeeze stroke, until the pressure built and erupted. The warm cloud of cum spurted onto his hand, washed away by the shower. He kept rubbing and squeezing until he was empty and could sag against the wall, body and mind cleared of tension, languid under the hot spray of water.

After that, Ryu took his time. Every moment spent in the shower was one less moment he had to face his seemingly hopeless situation. He'd had enough of bullies and their power over his life. Kiku had been the first person to see *him*, not what he could make of him. Everyone else wanted him to be something for them. An A student in a private school for his mother, a boxer and then a yak for his father, a sex slave for Taro Suzuki. Being a White Tiger was the only thing that he'd wanted for himself. He didn't even care if he went along with it to please Kiku who'd been everything to him for so long.

And now Kiku wasn't here.

Finally, afraid that Mega Cop might bang on the door and tell him to get out, Ryu turned off the shower and dried off. He tidied up the wet little cubicle as best he could and slipped his g-string back on, fully determined to get dressed the second he went out there. He didn't want any more accusations about seduction when all he'd been doing was desperately trying to make a point.

Hanging up his towel, he opened the door.

And froze.

Mega Cop stood in the doorway. No. Filled the doorway with his broad frame was more like it. Bare torso and a baggy pair of those pants they liked to wear in Thailand above his bare feet. His large eyes held a fierce determination. Full lips were pressed into a line.

Ryu's heart began to pump. His gaze moved over Phoenix's smooth chest, rounded muscles and hard stomach, all chiselled as if he'd been made from stone. The only indications he was flesh and blood were the deep caramel hue of his skin and the dark brown of his flat nipples.

Continuing down the length of one beefy arm, Ryu's look got trapped by the little machine in Phoenix's large hand.

A hair clipper.

No.

"Ryu."

Ryu whipped his head up, surprised that Phoenix had called him by his actual name. "Y…yes?"

"Time for a haircut."

Chapter Three

For a brief second, Miyazaki stood like a Sambar deer caught in a car's headlights.

Nat felt a pang but held his ground. The guy was getting a haircut. Now. "Look, if you just let me—"

"No."

"You're only making it harder for yourself." He hated using this typical cop line, but unfortunately for Miyazaki, it was true.

"I don't care. I can't cut my hair." Miyazaki sounded as if he were trying to give his voice a hard edge. It wasn't working. He sounded like a frightened kid putting on the tough act. One thing Nat sensed about the smaller man, he wasn't deep down tough. A tough guy would have already told him to fuck off.

Nat glanced down at Miyazaki's tattooed physique. In that split second his mind registered the perfect lean grace of his musculature underneath the myriad colours. Even the slopes of the man's thighs and calves displayed a kind of sculpted beauty that touched something inside him, made him feel that ache he always got when he wished his life were completely different than it was.

"Stop staring at me. I'm not a piece of meat."

Nat looked up, in time to see anger flash through Miyazaki's eyes. Suddenly, Miyazaki raised his fists, shifting his body into a fight stance. The grace and precision of his movement showed that he did indeed, know how to box.

Nat's heart pumped. Tension flooded his muscles. His thoughts flew from Miyazaki's beauty to the fact that the guy was willing to fight his way out of this haircut. Not that it was going to work. He was no match for Nat alone, never mind for Nat and Tongmee who stood to the side unseen, ready to pounce on Miyazaki and pin him on the bed so Nat could clip his hair.

The small room filled with the sound of tight breathing. Nat realised it wasn't his, but Miyazaki's. Each tight intake and exhale exuded the fear the smaller man was feeling and trying so obviously to hide. Nat decided to be as gentle as he possibly could.

He lunged. Fast.

A welterweight sized fist connected with his gut.

Nat let out a small whoosh of breath but wasn't hurt enough to stop. His arms shot out and caught Miyazaki up in a tight clinch.

Miyazaki grunted and rained his fists onto Nat's back. A smaller opponent would have taken quite a beating, but Nat's broadness absorbed the assault as if Miyazaki's fists were cotton balls landing on a rock.

Nat turned around and lunged through the doorway, depositing Miyazaki onto the bed on his back. Miyazaki's lean body twisted and writhed and he tried to pound his fists into Nat's face but Tongmee dashed over, grasped the flailing arms, and pinned them above Miyazaki's head.

"Hold him like that," Nat said. He straddled Miyazaki's hips, taking care not to crush him and flipped on the clippers. The tiny buzz was practically lost in the din of the air compressor of the window rattler and Miyazaki's yelps. "This won't take long, Ryu," he said.

Miyazaki pulled at his arms, held fast by Tongmee.

"Ah!" Miyazaki went stiff. He stopped struggling but his eyes widened with a look of terror. "Suzuki-san, *nanitozo!*"

Nat lowered the clippers and stopped.

"Suzuki-san, *nanitozo, nanitozo!*" Miyazaki's head began to thrash back and forth, his eyes seeming to be open as far as they could possibly go. The look in them made Nat feel as if he held a butcher's knife over the man instead of a harmless pair of safety clippers. "Suzuki-san, *nanitozo!*" Miyazaki's voice fell to a hush.

Nat felt a chill. Miyazaki spoke in rush of Japanese that he didn't understand, but he recognised the name Suzuki. He looked at Tongmee. "What's he saying?"

Tongmee was watching Miyazaki as if he'd sprouted three green heads. "He's saying, 'Suzuki-san, please, no, I beg you, don't. I won't tell my father. I promise.'"

Nat's blood went cold. He looked back down at Miyazaki. Tears slipped from the other man's eyes now, running silently down his cheeks as he repeated the same thing over and over. The room filled with his panicked breathy words and his eyes stared up, looking almost through Nat, as if Nat weren't there.

Shit. Miyazaki was in trauma.

Nat sprang off him and tossed the clippers to the floor. "Tongmee, let him go. Get off the bed now."

"What about his—"

"Now."

Tongmee released Miyazaki's arms and slid off the bed. "What the hell is his problem?"

The cruelty in Tongmee's tone struck him. "He's in trauma."

"He's crazy."

"Shut up, Agent Tongmee. He's a human being. Now get out of here and remain on stand-by."

"Yes sir." Tongmee glared at him and stalked out.

"Suzuki-san, *nanitozo! Nanitozo!*" Miyazaki's pleading voice still carried from the bed.

Nat turned around and froze. His heart threatened to lurch into his throat.

Though he and Tongmee had released him, Miyazaki remained in the same position, as if he were still being pinned down. His head still thrashed back and forth and his chest still heaved.

Nat drew closer and knelt on the edge of the bed. Was he faking? One quick look confirmed, no, he wasn't. Miyazaki's pupils were dilated, almost to the size of his irises in spite of the lights on in the room. There was no faking that. Shit, he and Tongmee had really done the wrong thing. "Ryu," he said softly. "Ryu."

Ryu didn't seem to hear him. He'd stopped thrashing his head, but he still stared up towards the ceiling, body in the same vulnerable position. "Taro-san, *nanitozo!*" Suddenly he cried out, a wail of pain. His hips shot up, knees bent.

Nat surged forward. "Ryu!" He reached out and put his hand over Ryu's forehead. The skin was warm and damp with sweat.

Just then, Nat's cell phone rang. He slid his hand back over Ryu's hair in a caress. He didn't want to leave Ryu, even to grab his phone, which he'd rested on top of the TV set when he changed clothes, but had to.

Sliding off the bed, he grabbed the cell phone and flipped it open. "Agent Phoenix."

"Agent Nat Phoenix?"

"Yes." Nat glanced over at the bed. Ryu was lying there quietly, still in the same position. The only thing moving was his chest as he panted.

"This is an interpreter for Kikuchiya Fujimara. May I proceed with the call?"

Nat's heart jumped. "Go ahead."

A short delay followed in which Nat could hear a man speaking in Japanese in the background.

"I'm calling to see how Ryu is. I sensed distress," the interpreter said in Thai.

Nat heaved a sigh. "Yes. He seems to be in a state of distress, a flashback of some sort. I'm sorry. I was trying to cut his hair. We had to restrain him, but something happened." During the delay that followed, Nat's fingers tightened on the phone. Guilt clawed at his chest. He lowered himself back onto the bed next to Ryu and stroked Ryu's hair, pink tips and all.

"I'm the one to apologise, Agent Phoenix," Fujimara said through the interpreter. "I wanted Ryu to dye out the colour before he left, but…he was…adamant about it and well, I felt so guilty towards him, I didn't push."

"Never mind that now. What's happening to him and how can I help him?" He looked down at Ryu while the interpreter spoke to Fujimara. Ryu's breathing had calmed a bit but his eyes were still wide, as if being stretched open beyond his control. Nat took hold of one wrist at a time and gently lowered Ryu's arms to his sides.

"Ten years ago, Taro Suzuki raped him."

"Fucking shit." Nat's blood felt cold in his veins.

"There were two of them. Suzuki and one of his goons. They held Ryu down in his own bed...in the middle of the night. I barged in and stopped them, but not soon enough."

Nat's vision blurred. The scene of a few moments ago replayed in his mind. Ryu's begging Suzuki to leave him alone, the way his hips lifted off the mattress, the cry of pain he let out, the glazed fear in his eyes...

Emotions swirled together in Nat, not the least of which was rage. Ryu was a wiry little guy, but two larger men had overpowered him in a matter of seconds. To think that someone...more than one...had used their strength to violate him. Fucking animals.

Nat wanted to throttle them, beat the shit out of them, but there was no one else there. Just him and Ryu.

"You should have told me this, Fujimara. It should have been in the case file so I would have known. I could have understood. I could have approached him differently." Ryu's responses to him made sense now. The poor guy. For what had happened to him, he'd been mostly easy to handle. It was just the thing with the hair...

He caressed Ryu's hair again, brushing his thumb across the damp skin of his forehead.

"You're absolutely right," Fujimara's interpreter said with almost no delay. "I can tell you how to bring him back now."

"Go ahead. I'll do anything." He rested his hand gently on Ryu's head, finding that he didn't want to break the contact.

"Tell him you're going to keep them away. Say it just like that. Then lie behind him and hold him."

Nat's skin prickled. "But I'm the one who got him into this state."

"That doesn't matter. If you're sincere with him...and gentle, he'll respond."

"I never would want to hurt him. I've been trying to protect him."

"I know, Agent Phoenix. Please call back later and let me know he's all right."

"I will. From now on, though, I need full disclosure from both of you. No secrets."

"No secrets."

Nat ended the call and set the phone on the floor by the bed. His heart hammered as he slid closer to Ryu. "Ryu," he said softly, "Fujimara…Kikuchiya told me to keep them away from you."

Ryu lay quietly now. His chest rose and fell in a more normal rhythm, but he remained unnaturally still, his gaze trained on the ceiling. He didn't even blink when Nat covered one bare shoulder and eased him onto his side. Ryu turned over as if he were a doll in Nat's hands.

"I'm sorry, Ryu. I'm very sorry. I didn't know. It'll be all right now." He squeezed Ryu's shoulder gently, relieved when Ryu didn't try to get away from him. "I'll keep them away from you, I promise." He pulled Ryu against him and spooned his back. Ryu's skin was warm against his chest.

Ryu was shivering now. Nat put one arm around him, resisting the sudden urge to press his lips to the back of Ryu's neck. Ryu's skin and hair smelled like sandalwood, exotic and sweetly clean at the same time. Nat closed his eyes and breathed in the scent, vibrantly aware of how perfectly Ryu's body fit to his. Ryu was about the size he and Aran had been when they were sixteen, just before Aran fell ill…

Another protective surge welled through Nat. "They can't hurt you now," he whispered, feeling his own breath pulse over Ryu's skin. He squeezed Ryu gently to emphasise his words. "I'm sorry, Ryu."

Ryu's shivering calmed a bit and Nat pressed his forehead to the back of Ryu's hair.

Suddenly, he felt a hand grasp his and hold on. His breath caught. Ryu's fingers slipped through his, lacing their hands together.

*He's a human being...I'm sorry, Ryu...I would never want to hurt him. I'm trying to protect him...*The words echoed through Ryu's mind, wearing down the edges of fear, softening the pain of memories.

He heaved a deep breath, allowing himself to relax into the warm strength surrounding him. The hand he squeezed, squeezed back and the tiny pulse of movement flooded him with a bit more safety.

The larger man's body heat penetrated his skin, calming the tremors that passed through him. He'd really been back there, back in his room. The weight on his arms and groin, the strength overpowering his, making him feel weaker and more helpless than an infant, had felt as real as when he was seventeen and Suzuki forced his dragon inside him. He'd been unable to stop the nightmare from flooding in, from nearly choking off his air, from begging Suzuki to stop, even though in some rational part of his mind, he knew Suzuki and Katsu weren't really there.

Especially when he'd begged and they *had* stopped. The men holding him had released him. One was angry. That Tongmee guy. Mean-spirited, that one. Emanated hatred, the way Suzuki did. But Phoenix...Nat...had defended him. The fighter he'd once admired and then come to see as a brute had shown the higher qualities Ryu had once thought he possessed all those times he'd watched him in the ring. The way Nat had told the mean guy to shut up and sent him out and had then caressed his head, so worried about him, had made Ryu able to let him hold him.

Ryu's eyelids fluttered as more tension drained from his limbs. A soft warm breath pulsed against the back of his neck, made him even more aware of the man holding him.

Made him aware of how long it had been since someone...since Kiku...had held him.

The sudden realisation made his hand tighten on Nat's. It really *had* been a long time, much longer than Ryu told himself it was. Several years before Yuzo had come around, Kiku had never let himself be pinned down to one man. Long before Yuzo, Kiku had stopped sharing his bed...

Fresh tears slipped from Ryu's eyes. Heartache flooded him from a deep invisible source, as if what had happened with Nat and the other agent had opened a door inside him, a place where he kept all his grief stuffed away. *Kuso*! The pain of seeing Kiku fall in love with someone else washed through him, as fresh and new as if it had just happened.

Ryu slipped his hand out of Nat's and turned over, pushing himself, face first, against Nat's broad warmth.

Nat's arms closed around him, pulled him into a tighter embrace. In the next second, Ryu felt a hand moving again over his hair. "I'm sorry, Ryu. I'm so sorry," he heard Nat whispering.

Ryu clutched at the other man's back. The muscles didn't give him much grip, but the hardness, warm and solid, felt real and reassuring under his hands, the way Kiku's had once felt. In the recess of his consciousness, he realised that Nat believed he was still in the trauma. Nat had no idea why he really was upset now, but Ryu couldn't explain. All he could do was feel, let his pain wash through him, comforted by the compassion surrounding him.

"I'm sorry I hurt you," Nat whispered.

The kind tone only spurred Ryu's tears, as if given permission to flow like a river. He'd cried like that with Kiku also, but it had been a long time ago, before Ryu became afraid to cry too much. Afraid that being inconsolable would eventually make Kiku abandon him, emotionally, the way his parents had. Maybe if he hadn't been so sad all the time, Kiku would have fallen in love with him.

"I'm sorry, Ryu."

Moments passed. Ryu tried to collect himself, to push the tears back down, but couldn't. They'd been stuffed down for too long and seemed to refuse his oppression. Only when they'd finally spent themselves, could he look up. Nat's rugged face was blurry through his tears but he smiled at him. "It's okay."

A gentle thumb brushed across his cheek, wiping the tears away. Nat's face was close to his, so close he could feel Nat's breath on his skin and smell his male scent, umasked by any cologne or strong soap.

"And I'm sorry I stared at you. I didn't mean to make you feel like a piece of meat."

Ryu froze at the sorrow in the man's voice. "It's okay. You didn't—"

"You just caught me by surprise. I didn't know you'd be so...beautiful."

Beautiful. No one had ever called him beautiful before, not even Kiku. Ryu blinked the tears from his eyes so he could see Nat's face more clearly.

The other man's huge brown eyes were watching him. He looked sad and worried. And sincere.

"Thank you, Nat," he whispered. Without thinking, his hand went to Nat's chest. What possessed him to lay his palm flat on the rounded muscle, he didn't know. The need to feel that hard warmth, the heart beating underneath, strong and reassuring. His own body felt cleansed, weary yet alive. And very aware of the other man's engulfing presence.

Ryu dared to trace his fingertips along Nat's collarbone. The larger man's skin was so smooth, so perfect. He followed the bone to the hollow of Nat's throat, tracing the rounded indentation before skimming back the way he'd come. He dipped his touch downward, just halfway, resisting his deep need to brush over the dark nipple a few inches away.

Nat's breath rose and fell, more deeply each passing moment. Ryu expected him to grasp his wrist and stop him any second now, but he didn't. He seemed to understand and silently let Ryu touch him.

This too, was like a memory, but a sweet one. Ryu thought of the way Kiku had let him run his hands over his powerful physique, allowed him to explore, to find pleasure. Even to touch and stroke Kiku's dragon, stopping any time he wanted to. But Kiku had been so gentle, he'd never wanted to stop. He wanted to stroke Nat's dragon now...

He slid his hand upward, over Nat's shoulder, and heard Nat's breath catch.

Caution showed in Nat's large eyes even though there seemed to be something else, too.

Ryu watched him, not sure whether to lift his hand away or not. "I'm not trying to seduce you, I swear." That accusation still resonated within him.

Nat exhaled and bowed his head. "I'm sorry I said that. Even if you are, it's okay." His fingertips brushed over Ryu's shoulder.

Ryu felt the man's potent yang simmer in the air. Nat's breathing was harsh and his nipples tight. These indications, mixed with the way Nat had stared had him and called him beautiful, let Ryu know that his touch was more than welcome.

Encouraged, he lifted his face up and pressed his lips to Nat's. His own breath caught at the contact with Nat's soft full lips. With the exception of that one last kiss with Kiku, kissing was something else he hadn't done in so long.

Nat stiffened and pulled away.

Immediately, Ryu's face burned and he looked down. "I'm sorry." Maybe he'd been wrong. Maybe he'd misread the signals and Nat really preferred women. Or just didn't prefer him. That wouldn't be a first. His mind blurred and he started to turn over.

But a hand on his arm stopped him. "Don't do that." Gentle pressure eased him onto his back.

Nat pulled in a deep breath. His thoughts were incoherent, as if the blood thundering through his body had drained from his mind. He'd wanted to deepen the kiss but still felt like a brute, unworthy of the sudden trust Ryu was giving him. "I just don't want to be like…" The rest of his sentence stuck in his throat.

"Like what?" Ryu's voice was nearly a whisper. His breathing too, was harsh like Nat's.

Nat restrained himself from lowering his mouth down to Ryu's again. The way the other man was looking up at him, eyes wide and soft, red-rimmed from crying but also dusky was one of the sweetest yet most erotic things he'd ever seen. Damn. If he'd prayed to Buddha for a more beautiful man, he couldn't have found one. Especially one who fit so perfectly in his arms, body hard and lean yet also pliant. "I don't want to be like Suzuki."

Ryu's lips parted and a sheepish look stole through his eyes. He exhaled sharply then turned his head away. "Kiku told you."

"Yes. I should have been told from the beginning. I would have handled this whole hair thing differently."

Ryu tried to turn again, but Nat kept a hand on his shoulder. He loved that warm colourful skin. "It's okay, Ryu."

"No, it's not. I should be over it by now. It happened ten years ago."

"It doesn't work that way." He reached out and brushed his thumb across Ryu's cheek. Resting his hand there, he traced the round contour of the other man's cheekbone. How many times had he thought the same thing about his own grief? After twenty-one years, he missed his brother as much as he had when Aran first died.

Ryu's long lashes moved as he blinked. His face turned against Nat's hand and his innocent gaze was trained upward. "I wish it did."

Nat smoothed Ryu's hair back. "Me too."

Ryu looked back up at him. His soft lips parted and Nat felt the silent invitation. Ryu's hand lifted and cupped the back of his neck. "You'd stop if I wanted you to, right?"

Heat zinged through Nat's gut, tingling all the way into his already painfully tight cock. "Of course I would."

Ryu's eyes lit up and he smiled. In the next second, Nat felt the hand on his neck gently pulling him down…

Chapter Four

This time, Nat let himself be pulled down. He closed his lips over Ryu's...and nearly lost his mind. So soft and yielding, Ryu parted for him, inviting him to taste deeply. Nat groaned and slipped one hand into Ryu's hair. His fingers raked easily through the hot pink spikes to cradle the back of his head while he stroked Ryu's tongue with his.

Ryu's arms closed around him and caressed him as they kissed. Ryu's fingertips and palms glided over the span of his back then down the muscles along his spine, like feathers against his skin, only a hell of a lot better. Each time, the other man's touch skated just to the waistband of Nat's pants and hesitated, as if wanting to go further, then slid back up again.

Nat groaned and deepened the kiss. Ryu's mouth remained softly open, accepting every lick and nip of his tongue and lips. As always, Ryu's woodsy scent surrounded him, diffused by the heat of their bodies pressed together. In the haze of his mind, Nat felt a bit oafish, like his kisses were clumsy and rough. But Ryu opened his lips wider and answered the swirl of Nat's tongue with his. Which was a damn good thing because he was delicious beyond compare.

Time and space blurred. All Nat's awareness funnelled down to Ryu's wiry body warm and yielding against his, the sweet taste of his mouth and the flood of need in his own body. Pulling his mouth from their kiss, he licked and nibbled his way over Ryu's jaw, down his throat to his chest.

Ryu's hands slipped from his back with the movement and cradled his head. Nat could hear the tiny whimpers of pleasure each time his tongue connected with Ryu's bare skin. The man's flesh was salty sweet, like the most delicious treasure. If Nat had imagined the colours on his skin as separate tastes, he'd been wrong. The white tigers and the swirls of colour around them all had the same delectable flavour. Ryu.

Ryu. Ryu. Ryu. The name swam around in his mind, filled it as he filled his taste buds with the warm skin hugging Ryu's chest muscles. Eyes closed, Nat savoured every inch, brushing his tongue over him as delicately as he could. At Ryu's nipple, he slowed down more, feeling the smooth skin tighten, savouring the musky flavour, hearing Ryu pull in a breath and whisper his name with his fingers clutched into Nat's hair.

Nat slid his hand from Ryu's hair and explored him. What he really wanted to do was pull down that g-string and taste everything he'd seen bulging through the pouch of cloth earlier, but held back. Knowing what he did now, he couldn't possibly unleash all his lust onto Ryu without feeling like an evil beast. Instead, he let his fingertips slide gently up and down Ryu's arm. Ryu's hands still cradled his head and Nat traced the way that position made his lean muscles flex, appreciated the cords of muscle in his forearms under the soft hairs.

Only then did he let himself touch more. His hand closed softly around the side of Ryu's waist.

Ryu moaned and released a soft whoosh of breath. The sound reminded Nat of the other man's incredible lips. He lifted his head and took them again, dipping his tongue deeply into that delicious, warm, yielding place. Ryu moaned again, an easy vibration Nat felt in his own mouth.

Nat let his hand slide down, over Ryu's hip down his leg. Every inch of this man was warm smooth skin and lean muscle. He squeezed Ryu's thigh, just above the knee, kneading and caressing, feeling his way upward over the slope of muscle, around to Ryu's inner thigh, carefully, making sure his exploring fingers were never uninvited. He dared to let his fingertips graze the underside of Ryu's balls over the cloth of the g-string. He tensed a bit, wondering if that had been the right thing to do, but in the next second Ryu groaned. His legs fell open and his tongue surged against Nat's, as if silently demanding more.

One of Ryu's hands left his hair. Nat felt the fingers close around his wrist. His breath caught softly. Had he gone too far? Too close to the part of Ryu that had once been violated? But instead of pulling him away, he found his fingers being guided under the cloth, felt his palm graze Ryu's hard cock and over the firm sac below. Ryu exhaled sharply into Nat's mouth and his hips rose, pushing his erection more firmly against Nat's hand.

Nat groaned again. His body surged and the same flush of pleasure in his chest he'd felt upon meeting Ryu in the airport fanned through his entire body. Carefully, he kneaded the sac, earning a groan with each pulse of his fingertips. He squeezed gently, then let his palm slide up and down along Ryu's cock. Each stroke of his hand over the velvety skin and hard muscle made him wilder.

Pulling himself back, he eased the g-string away, trying hard not to yank it down Ryu's slim hips. Nat didn't want to do anything that smacked of aggression. Not that he'd ever been a rough lover with anyone. Nor had he ever felt so completely...so strangely...aware...of every breath, every nuance of feel and scent.

Suddenly Ryu was helping him pull down the g-string, bending his knees and working it over his ankles until he could toss it away. Nat broke their kiss and looked down. The sight of Ryu's cock curving upward from his slim, hard body made Nat's mouth water. Staring at the trail of dark hair from Ryu's bellybutton to his pubic hair, Nat wanted nothing more than to stroke every part of him, to lean over and suck off the drop of cum that had seeped from the plump head of his cock.

"I know. I'm not...big." Ryu's dark eyelashes fluttered downward and he shifted his head away.

Nat brushed his fingertips on Ryu's cheek, using gentle pressure to turn him back. The other man's eyes reflected deep shyness, but through Nat's lust-heated mind, he couldn't follow. "What do you mean?"

"My dragon. It's...small."

"Dragon?"

Ryu blinked. "Yes." He pointed downward. "My dragon." He cleared his throat. "I think you find it small." His voice ended on a whisper and again he looked down again.

Only then did Nat realise his hesitancy had been mistaken for something else. "Damn, I couldn't care less about the size of your...um...dragon." He couldn't help grinning at the strange terminology, but fell serious again when he saw the look on Ryu's face. The guy genuinely needed reassurance, he realised. He took Ryu's cock in his palm and closed his fingers around it. Ryu wasn't hung like an elephant, but he was just right. Everything about him was...amazing. He grinned. "It fits the rest of you perfectly." He stroked up the length, making Ryu pull in a breath. "See?" Ryu's eyelids shuttered and he breathed harshly. Nat stroked down the other way. Damn, the velvet skin over hard cock was something he hadn't felt in so long. "Perfect." He rubbed again.

"Ohhh." Ryu's lips were parted and he stared up at Nat, his dark irises glazed again, but not in that horrible way like before.

Nat started an easy rhythm of stroking now, from the base of Ryu's cock to the head. He continued to stare down at Ryu as he rubbed. Ryu's eyes were wide, but simmering and the corners of his lips turned up now. Even though his own cock was tight to the point of pain, he found himself captured in that gaze, appreciating everything he saw in it, including a vulnerable human being. "See, Ryu? You fit just right in my hand."

As he spoke and stroked him, Ryu's smile deepened. His head fell back and his hips moved, just enough to push against the rhythm of Nat's hand. Nat stroked a bit faster. Ryu groaned. Suddenly, he rolled into Nat's front and in the next second, Nat felt hands on his back pulling him down again.

The movement made their cocks brush together. Nat closed their lips together as the heat spilled through his groin. The coarse linen of his pants rubbed his cock, sending more sparks through him. The moist heat of Ryu's tongue against his sent his last bit of control spiralling away. He surged over Ryu, covering him and thrust against him.

Ryu's fingers suddenly gripped his upper arms and Ryu broke their kiss. "Too rough," he breathed.

Nat quickly raised himself on one arm. "I'm sorry." Shit, he'd gotten too carried away.

Ryu smiled again. "Not you. I meant these." He lowered his hand and tugged on Nat's pants.

Relief prickled through him. Without hesitation, he pulled the string tie and the gathered material at the waist fell open. In the next second, Ryu's hands grasped the excess and pushed it past Nat's hips. His freed cock sprang out, only to be captured and immediately rubbed.

Nat pulled in a breath. His vision blurred a bit from the grip of pleasure, but didn't blot out the need burning in Ryu's dark irises. Ryu didn't seem to feel forced at all.

Without thinking, Nat closed his body over Ryu's again. With no barrier between them, their cocks slid easily together encased in Ryu's hand.

The contact was like a continuous hot current of electricity down the length of his body. He took deep gasping breaths, trying to slow down, not to ride him furiously, even as he was desperate for release, but couldn't. Ryu was just too…damn…perfect.

Ryu stared up at him, barely blinking. His soft lips opened and closed with each slide of their cocks together.

Nat reminded himself to take it easy. He scanned Ryu's face, making sure that the glazed look on his rounded features remained one of enjoyment. One of Ryu's hands rested on Nat's back and the sensation of those fingertips on his lat muscle sent a primal feeling through him, a possessive fervour for the man underneath him.

The emotion curled through his insides, fuelled his movements even as it unnerved him. Gripping the pillow on either side of Ryu's head, he braced his upper body and increased the mind–blowing friction by stroking faster.

The window rattler shut off in that moment and the sounds of his and Ryu's harsh breaths filled his ears. Ryu moaned softly then tilted his head upward. His eyes rolled back in his head and his fingers pressed into Nat's skin, followed by the warm splash of cum between them.

Nat looked down at the milky cloud that muted the colours on Ryu's stomach.

"Don't stop, Nat," Ryu whispered. His eyes were closed but his hand remained on their cocks, holding them together. "I want you to come too."

The feverish plea made Nat so hot, he obeyed immediately. The cum seeping out made him glide even more intensely against Ryu. The pressure built hard and fast until he erupted.

Ryu's other hand slid up and cupped the back of his neck. "Kiss me," he whispered. His lips were soft and full from arousal and the scent of musky sex and sandalwood filled the air around their sweating bodies.

Another sweet shiver passed through Nat and he obeyed again. Ryu stroked his emptying cock with his hand as their lips met and parted. Nat swirled his tongue against Ryu's while waves of release ploughed through him.

He shuddered with the last tremors of climax then gently collapsed. Ryu's hand slipped away and his arms closed again around Nat's torso. Sweat and cum fused their skin together but Nat didn't care. His mind and body felt deliciously empty, as if the entire world and all its problems had faded. The only things that existed were, Ryu underneath him, soft breath pulsing against his skin as Ryu's hands caressed his back.

After a few minutes, Nat shifted slightly. He'd never been able to rest still for any length of time his entire life. Worry was always nagging at him, a constant companion he first knew when Aran had fallen ill and stayed even after his beloved brother had died. He pressed his lips to Ryu's shoulder as the sweet languor he'd felt slipped away.

Truthfully, he'd never had sex he'd considered sweet...until this moment. As sweet as it was hot. It made him wish...so many things, not the least of which that Ryu didn't already belong to another guy...

Nat exhaled. He'd really fucked up now. "Damn!"

Ryu tensed underneath him and his hands stilled their caressing. "What's wrong?"

Nat levered carefully upward, away from that delicious, sinewy body. Cool air passed through the space between them and he longed to lie back down. But couldn't. He looked into Ryu's eyes, sorry at the renewed alarm in them. "This shouldn't have happened," he murmured. "I...wasn't thinking straight. You're just so damn hot." The words spilled from him, uncharacteristic compliments. Not that he was never appreciative. He just didn't usually say such things out loud.

Ryu's hands slipped down to the mattress. Guilt stole over his flushed face and he turned his face to the side. "I'm sorry. It's my fault."

"No. It's not you. I...took advantage. Of the situation. I'm supposed to be taking care of you. Not...this." He sat up and raked a hand through his damp hair. "I'm going to have to tell Fujimara the truth. If he wants another agent on the case instead of me I'll understand."

Ryu's eyes widened and he now looked at him. "Kiku? He won't want someone else. Neither do I. I'll tell him. When I call him. He'll want to know I'm all right."

A mournful feeling sat in the pit of his gut. What a day this had been. In a space of hours he'd gone from seeing Ryu as an amoral brat, a pink-haired weirdo covered with tattoos, to the hottest man he'd ever gone to bed with and who felt so perfect in his arms he couldn't believe it. Of course, it figured that on top of all that, Ryu was another man's lover. He hadn't been convinced that Ryu and Fujimara were lovers, but now, after this taste of the man, he couldn't imagine that Fujimara wasn't all over Ryu, all the time. No wonder the guy was going to such pains and expense to keep Ryu safe. "All right. You tell him. I'm sorry. I hope this doesn't…damage your relationship."

"Damage our relationship?" Ryu sounded genuinely puzzled. "Me and Kiku?"

Nat's heartbeat sped up a bit. "Yeah. You're lovers, aren't you?"

"No."

His gaze whipped to Ryu's. "You're not?"

The other man still lay against the pillow, returning his look. The expression in his eyes was strange, a mixture of confusion and sadness. "Kiku and I aren't lovers." His tone was soft, hard to distinguish the emotions in it. "We were…a long time ago." Ryu sighed and directed his gaze towards the ceiling. "But it's been years."

For a moment he was silent and Nat watched him, suddenly at a terrible loss for words. He wanted to enjoy the intense, delightful relief he felt at that admission, but something about Ryu's demeanour held him back.

Ryu must have taken Nat's silence as a demand for more information because he turned over and propped his head on his elbow, a resolved expression on his face. "I know. No secrets. In spite of the state I was in, I heard what you said to Kiku on the phone."

Nat wanted to stop him, tried to say the words that would let Ryu know this was something he didn't need to divulge. Perhaps it was morbid curiosity that kept him silent, like an itch he just needed to scratch…to know all he could about Ryu…for himself.

"After what happened with Suzuki, Kiku took me in. He let me stay with him. I just couldn't live at home, in my room, after that."

Nat lowered himself down, onto one elbow so that he faced Ryu. Close enough that he could reach out and touch him, but far back enough to give him space. "Didn't your father know?"

Ryu shook his head. His look of sadness deepened. "I didn't want Kiku to tell him. I don't know how much you know about *yakuza*, but they're not exactly family-oriented, like...*The Sopranos*. The crime family comes first, before wife and kids. I don't believe my father would have punished Suzuki. I don't think he would have believed I didn't do anything to make it happen. I would have probably just been sent away to boarding school or something."

"What about your mom?"

Ryu sighed. "My mom was trafficked from Thailand to be a whore. It just so happened she was my dad's favourite and he ended up marrying her. Her life is all about survival. She wouldn't have the power to do anything about Suzuki. She would have been afraid of getting us killed." Pain clouded Ryu's beautiful eyes. "While Suzuki and his goon were on top of me, she was serving a midnight feast to the others out in the living room. Who knows? She may even have seen Suzuki head towards my room."

Before he realised what he was doing, Nat reached out and covered Ryu's shoulder. "I'm sorry."

Ryu looked down and Nat could sense his embarrassment and grief. "Thanks. Anyway, I lived with Kiku after that. He didn't ask anything of me, but I...threw myself at him."

Nat stared. He couldn't imagine this beautiful guy needing to throw himself at anyone. But in that moment, he had an intense vision of Ryu, younger, maybe even before dying his hair and getting tattooed, desperate for attention and affection.

When Ryu raised his face again, Nat could see the pain of the memories. He was sorry he hadn't stopped Ryu from speaking about it, but even now, couldn't. He just *had* to know.

"Kiku let me be with him. He wanted me to heal, so I wouldn't go crazy or something. I know he loves me. He just was never *in* love with me. Not with anyone. But I know how important I am to him because he left the *yakuza* for *me*. He didn't want to be a hypocrite. When I started getting the tattoos, he begged me to stop. I was doing it to show him I could be tough and strong too, and I wanted to have them because he had them. But he was convinced I would end up a criminal and didn't want me to become a yak, so he left, even though it meant *yubizume*."

Nat knew the term. Finger-cutting. He'd learned about that custom when studying organised crime during police training. A guy who wanted to leave the *yakuza* cut off a piece of his finger to mark himself as a former mobster. Or, if he'd insulted a higher up, he gave the piece of finger as an apology.

Ryu huffed. "Yeah. Ironic, isn't it? He ended up giving the finger to Suzuki who took his place. By then though, Kiku had already started with the White Tiger path. He used to go to Shanghai on business and met some guy there who got him into it. When he went legit, he turned his gambling parlour into the hotel, to make money while he studied. Now there's a group of us who help Kiku run the place while we practice."

For a few moments, Ryu didn't speak and the only sound in the room was his soft breathing. "And then," he went on finally, "not long ago, Kiku fell in love. With another victim of Suzuki's perversions. Yuzo came running to the White Tiger, trying to get away from Suzuki and this time, Kiku lost his heart. And then another part of his finger. As an apology for stealing what had belonged to Suzuki." Ryu's disgust was evident in his tone.

He exhaled and looked at Nat. Anger and sadness tinged his eyes and it was clear that although Ryu and Fujimara weren't lovers anymore, the arrangement hadn't been agreeable to Ryu. "Suzuki wanted me in trade for Yuzo. That's why Kiku sent me away. Now you know the whole story."

Nat frowned. "I thought it was because you refused to throw a fight."

Ryu nodded. "I did refuse to throw a fight. Because Kiku begged me not to do it when I told him what Taro wanted. When we told Suzuki I wasn't going to throw the fight, Suzuki said he'd take me in trade for other purposes than boxing. Of course, you probably can figure out what *that* means." His eyes seemed to study Nat's, and understanding came into them, as if he'd guessed the question forming in Nat's mind. "I know, you want to ask me, 'why not just throw the fight if it would have pacified Suzuki and prevented this from happening?'"

"I was going to ask that."

The other man gave a choked laugh. "Because! Nothing will pacify Suzuki for more than five minutes. Nothing. So Kiku didn't want me to lose my dignity on top of everything else, if we were going to have a problem with Taro anyway. I was happy to refuse to let myself get knocked out when I had a chance at winning. Even though it meant not boxing anymore." Ryu looked at him and for the first time, Nat saw fierce pride. "Suzuki has gotten enough from me," he said in a dark tone. "At least I have a shred of dignity."

Nat squeezed Ryu's arm gently. "I agree," he said, though it pained him to see how much Ryu had lost because of that sadistic bastard. He wanted to pull Ryu into his arms again, but suddenly felt as if he couldn't. What had just happened between them had been a momentary comfort, but Ryu was obviously still in love with Fujimara and Nat was not going to take advantage of him. "Thank you for trusting me with your story."

Ryu looked at him as if he'd said a ridiculous thing. "What choice do I have, Nat? My life is not my own. It never has been. If you tell me I need to give you full disclosure in order to protect me from a killer, I'll do it. Besides, when I tried to make my own decision, it didn't go so well." He pointed to his hair.

Guilt spiked through Nat at that statement, both from the reference to Ryu's hair and for the way he'd just tricked Ryu. True, there were parts of Ryu's story that were helpful to him as a cop, but he couldn't excuse the other parts, the personal things Nat had wangled from him under false pretences. "I'm sorry. Maybe one day it'll change."

Ryu's shoulders sagged. "That's what I tell myself." He was silent a moment then looked back up. "Any other questions?"

Nat returned that dark gaze. It was all he could do not to get completely lost in it. He had a million questions, but didn't know if he'd ever get to ask them. "Not right now."

Ryu nodded. "Okay."

"Well, just one."

"Yeah?"

Nat smiled at him. "Are you hungry? It's almost night time and you've barely eaten. Maybe you'd like to get out of here and walk on the beach?"

Ryu's eyebrows rose. "I thought I wasn't supposed to leave the room."

Nat's heart jumped. He remembered the things he'd said to Ryu...when he hadn't known the truth. Damn. If he could take back every last word, he would. "You could wear the hat, tonight. I guess."

"No. It's okay." Ryu raked his fingers through the pink spikes. He sat up and bowed his head. "Where are those clippers?"

Chapter Five

Tokyo, Japan

"Doing it again, are you, Fujimara? Hiding one of your precious boys so I can't get to him?" Suzuki chuckled. The sound was menacing to Kiku's ears. Evil.

Kiku's hand tightened on his phone. Did the yak on the other end have even *one* redeeming quality? If so, he managed to keep it so well hidden as to be nonexistent. "You'll never touch Ryu again. Not while I'm alive."

Apparently, Suzuki had called for Ryu while Kiku was out. Good thing Naoto had answered. He was a tough kid, unafraid of Suzuki and able to handle him.

Suzuki gave that skin-crawling laugh again. "You've always tried to play tough, haven't you, Fuju? For some reason years ago, Suzuki had nicknamed him Fuju. Knowing Taro, it was probably some sort of perverse affection. "But it's all bluster with you. In the end, you try to please everyone. It will be your downfall."

"I was tough enough to get you off poor Ryu's ass. Without a fight."

At that, Suzuki's fury sizzled through the line. Hurt pride was the only thing that really angered the yak. Kiku had seen that for years. Far more than Suzuki's desire for money, pride was the tragic flaw that motivated everything he did. It was Suzuki's injured pride that had sparked and sustained this battle between them for the last thirteen years.

"You think I took Ryu's virginity in order to prove some point?" He laughed in a way that made Kiku's skin erupt in gooseflesh. "I know you believe that, Fuju. Your simpleton's mind reduced my act of passion to an act of revenge on Naboru for stealing my father's regard from me. You're wrong. Ryu is the finest piece of ass in Tokyo. There's no one else like him. No one. He makes Yuzo look like a piece of dog shit and has twice the brains."

Kiku's heart lurched. Of course it had been about revenge, anger. Suzuki had wanted to violate Ryu, to exert power over him and show Ryu's father that he really had the upper hand. Still, Suzuki's way of speaking, his certainty that what he'd done was from passion or some affection for Ryu made his gut clench. Hard. The hand that held the phone sweated, almost making the receiver slip away. He clutched it, resisting with all his strength not to throw it down and go do the one thing he'd sworn never to do to another human being. Murder.

But Suzuki wasn't human.

"Surprised you, didn't I, Fuju? You think I'm a killing machine with no feelings."

"You *have* no conscience."

"No conscience, eh? That's why I gave you a deadline of ten days for your finger after the insult you dealt me with Yuzo? You're not even one of us anymore. I could simply have shot you instead of asking a mild payback. No conscience? That's why in spite of my feelings about Ryu, I never demanded to have him when I came to

your place, never threatened you or any one of your boys even though I knew you'd hidden Ryu away until I left? Let me tell you one thing, Fuju, you think you're smart and strong, but the only reason you and your precious boys are alive is because of my conscience."

"What conscience is it that rapes a boy and then later destroys his career, won't let him have a moment's peace because you find his body pleasing? You're a sadistic bastard."

"Come now, Fuju. Be honest. You didn't want to see Ryu's beautiful face get all marked up and toughened anymore than I did."

"You felt the same about his tender asshole, didn't you?"

For several moments the only response was Suzuki's breathing and Kiku could feel the other man trying to control his temper. "You'll never hide him far enough away Fuju. Before this is over, you'll see his naked body against mine. That's a promise."

"Fuck you." Kiku slammed the button down and tossed the phone to the polished dark wood of the floor. He put his head in his hands and slumped over, elbows on his knees, his fingers agitating in circles against his shaved scalp. *I'm cracking,* he thought. He'd never let Suzuki get to him this way before, never let him get the upper hand the way he had in this conversation. All these years, trying to hold all their lives together, struggling to keep his White Tigers safe and still honour all his promises of silence to the organisation were wearing him down. The problem with straddling a fence was,it became impossible not to slip and impale oneself on a spike.

"It's my karma," he murmured out loud. He'd been a criminal, lain with pigs and so he'd ended up in the mud with them. Even a few of the others, like Naoto, had fought on the streets, stolen, acted as messengers for the yaks. But Ryu? What bad had he ever done to anyone?

He remembered seeing Ryu at the Miyazakis' house when he'd go there, walking around at age ten in his private school uniform. He looked sad and a bit sullen, but never hurt anyone. Got good grades, obeyed his parents. The only time Kiku had ever seen Ryu smile was when *he* came over. That's when he'd realised it, Ryu's admiration for him. Being the light of a kid's life was a rare privilege, and one he'd tried to honour ever since. Though most of the time he did a piss-poor job of it.

"Kiku."

He didn't look up at the sound of Yuzo's voice. He couldn't bring himself to look at the younger man. Yuzo, Ryu, all of them, they put so much faith in him and all he did was sit on the fence, just as Suzuki had accused him. That was the one thing Taro had correct. He tried to please everyone and the problem only grew worse, so much worse that Ryu was all the way in Thailand. With strangers.

A hand closed over one knee. "Kiku."

"Not now."

Yuzo's hand slipped away, but he remained kneeling.

The gesture pricked Kiku's guilt and he lifted his gaze. Yuzo too, wore an expression of intense guilt. Kiku reached out and touched his cheek. "I'm sorry."

"It's my fault. All of this, isn't it?"

"Stop talking about fault." He heaved a deep sigh and sat up. "We're dealing with a complete psychopath. This began before you were even born."

Yuzo nodded. He rose up on his knees and leaned forward. "What can I do to help?"

Kiku stared back at him. *Help? What could anyone do to help?* His own weaknesses and misguided sense of honour had deepened the mess they were in, just like in that Shakespeare play he'd once read, where the prince of Denmark stewed in his own indecision until he went mad... Perhaps if he'd gone to Naboru Miyazaki in the first place and told him Suzuki had raped his son, something would have been done sooner. Perhaps if he'd been willing to testify and tell the cops of that murder he'd witnessed Suzuki commit last winter, Suzuki could have been stopped. Or...

His heart lurched and he reached out, grasping Yuzo's arms. The sudden force of resolve nearly took his breath away. "I need one thing from you."

Yuzo's large eyes widened. "Anything, Kiku."

Realising the strength of his grip on the smaller man's arms, he eased his hold. "Two things, actually."

"Anything."

"First, stand by me, whatever happens."

"Always. And the other?"

Kiku stared into the deep brown irises looking back at him. "Pray that I've earned enough good karma to turn our fortune."

Phuket, Thailand

"All right. Go ahead." Ryu squeezed his eyes shut, body tense.

The clipper buzzed ominously when Nat flicked the button and Ryu suppressed a rush of tears. His hands clenched on his thighs and he caught his breath when Nat stepped closer and moved the buzzer over the top of his hair.

Whoosh. Like a breeze through cherry blossoms, the clipper ruffled his hair. Ryu dared to open his eyes and saw the pink clippings tumble, landing on the floor and on the towel, spread underneath him on the bed. Like cherry blossoms falling in the breeze.

Nat's hand followed the clipper in a caress, brushing away the cut wisps. The buzzing sound rose and fell with its arc over Ryu's hair, pink locks raining around him until he was sure he'd end up bald.

Panic rose, making his chest tighten mercilessly. A vision of wandering, lost, through a city, his hair shorn, assaulted his mind. He fought to control his breath. He saw Kiku, soaring over head, unable to find him because he blended into the crowds. Ryu looked up and called to him, flailing his arms and jumping up and down, to no avail. Kiku passed over and disappeared...

The clipper shut off. "Ryu?" Gentle fingertips lifted his chin.

Only then did he realise he was breathing in that anxious way he had when he was panicked. "I'm all right. I'm sorry. And I'm sorry I punched you before."

Nat's gaze came even with his as the other man knelt in front of him. "It's all right."

"No it's not. I shouldn't have been so difficult."

Nat's hand closed over his shoulder and squeezed. His large eyes showed genuine concern. "I'm sure there was a good reason."

"It's a babyish reason."

Nat furrowed his brow. "I wouldn't be so quick to judge it."

Ryu's heartbeat sped up more. Nat seemed willing to let it drop. He certainly wasn't pressing for an explanation. So why did it feel so urgent to tell him the truth? "I dyed it in the first place so Kiku could always find me, no matter where I was or how many people were around." There, he'd admitted it. He tensed, waiting for Nat to laugh at him.

Instead, Nat's thumb brushed across his shoulder. "I understand."

"You do?" Relief prickled down his arms, especially through the spot where Nat's hand rested.

Nat nodded. "Yes." He breathed a heavy sigh. "I know what it means to live your life in a certain way because of bad things that happened." He gave Ryu's shoulder a quick squeeze and released him. "My whole boxing career was like that." Raw emotion passed quickly across Nat's rugged face. "I guess it's only fair to share something personal with you since you spilled your guts to me before."

Ryu could only stare at him, wondering at how Nat had gone from being Mega Cop to this nice guy in so short a time. "You don't have to. Tell me something so private, I mean."

"I had a brother. An identical twin. Aran. We both wanted to be professional boxers, or at least Muay Thai fighters. When we were sixteen, he drank some bad water…in the rice paddy on our parents' farm. A dead animal or something got into it. Aran got really sick and nothing would make him better." He looked down and Ryu could feel his grief pulsing in the air around them, as potent as his yang force had been earlier. "Everything I've done after that was for him. Boxing, becoming a cop. All of it. As if, somehow, it would keep me closer to him."

Nat's heart pumped and the hand holding the clippers trembled. When he looked up again, Ryu's dark eyes were misted over and he was frowning.

"That's awful, Nat. I'm sorry."

Nat sighed. He hadn't wanted to talk about Aran only because it hurt so damn much even to say his name. But after the way he'd tricked Ryu into telling him such personal things, it was the only way he knew to make amends.

"Thanks." He ran a hand over Ryu's hair, checking for stray pink. There was none. "You're all set. I'll get this cleaned up while you dress." He had already tied his fisherman pants back on before clipping Ryu's hair but Ryu still sat naked on the towel.

"I'll help you." Ryu stood up and then knelt down, brushing wisps of his hair together into a small pile on the tile floor.

Nat lifted the towel carefully and had Ryu put the pile onto the already hair-filled towel. "I'll shake this out outside." He waited a moment for Ryu to pull on a pair of baggy pants from his duffel bag before opening the door and tried to ignore the spike of guilt through his chest as the pants covered Ryu's thighs and ass. What he was feeling guilty about, he wasn't sure, considering there were several poignant reasons, not the least of which was his disappointment that Ryu was no longer completely naked.

He went out the door to the corner where Lew always kept a large trash can. Setting aside the lid, he let the towel drop open and shook the pink wisps into the garbage.

"So, you got the kid to lose the electric hair."

Nat looked up to see Tongmee saunter over to him. The slim man wore an expression that made him look like he'd just swallowed sour milk. "You have some powers of persuasion, Agent Phoenix."

A flash of anger made Nat's chest feel suddenly cold. "What are you getting at, Tongmee?"

Tongmee leaned a shoulder against the side of the building, arms crossed in front of him. "I mean, I've been keeping watch outside the room and it's amazing what you can hear once the window rattler goes silent."

Nat's heart lurched and his fists tightened on the towel. An angry rejoinder hovered on his lips but he held back and took a deep breath. Tongmee had never really been what one could call a nice guy, but he'd always been a good, reliable agent, devoted to his work. At least from what Nat could see. Tongmee was busted up from his brother's death, and this was certainly something Nat could understand. Even if his own way of dealing with Aran's death had not been to take refuge in some perverse form of hatred. "Look, Tongmee, this case...it seems bad timing for you. If you need some time off, or a transfer back to Bangkok, it's all right. Really, I'll call it in for you."

Nat saw his words hit some sort of mark in the other man, even though manipulation hadn't been his intention.

Tongmee started and stood away from the wall. His pinched features eased a bit. "No. No need for that. I...I was out of line. I'll...um...stay. I've always finished a job."

"I know. It's just that you've been under so much stress. I just wanted to help."

"Thanks."

Nat's hands eased on the towel and he folded it loosely as he told Tongmee the plans for the evening. "You stay back here with Pettoh. I need two men to keep watch while we're out."

Tongmee bowed his head. "All right." He lifted his face and stood, obviously waiting to be dismissed.

"Go ahead." Nat watched the other agent turn the corner to continue his surveillance. Tongmee seemed much calmer now, as if what Nat had said to him had delivered a small shock. Well, maybe it had, but the distraction from Tongmee's grief could only last so long. The ghosts always returned to haunt. With a sigh, he turned and went back into the room.

The second he walked in, the energy was different. Immediately he recognised the soft energy of meditation and clicked the door shut as quietly as he could.

Ryu had straightened up the bed and sat in front of his pillow, legs folded in lotus posture. He still wore the baggy pants he'd put on before and wore an equally baggy tunic with sleeves long enough to cover his tattoos. He opened his eyes and turned. When their gazes met, a sheepish look shadowed his face, as if he'd been caught stealing. "I'm sorry."

Why was he apologising for meditating? "I can go back outside if you need—"

"I don't. Will you come sit with me?"

The question sent a flush of warmth through Nat's chest, almost dispelling the uneasy feeling Tongmee had left him with. He nodded and walked over to the bed. Settling next to Ryu and folding his legs into lotus posture, he was finding awfully quickly that it was difficult to refuse this man anything. "It's been a while since I meditated." To his shame, the last time he'd meditated was the last time his parents had sent him and Aran to meditation camp at the local Buddhist temple, as they'd done every summer until…

"No problem."

Nat looked at him. Without the pink hair, Ryu's face looked even more beautiful than it had before. And then he noticed something else. "You took out the nose ring," he said, relieved that he wasn't going to have to ask Ryu to do that.

Ryu nodded. That sad look he had often, now returned. "Yes. I knew it had to come out. Kiku wanted me to remove it before I left. I should have listened to him."

Truthfully, he looked better without that too, but Nat remained quiet. From what he'd learned of this man, Ryu had a symbolic reason for everything he did. Considering the usual meaning of a gold ring, as well as the reverent tone he always used when he spoke of Fujimara, it wasn't hard to figure out what that meant. "Thank you," was all he could say.

Ryu nodded and turned back to meditation. He closed his eyes and rested his hands, one on the other, palms up, just in front of his middle.

Nat placed himself into the posture the monks had taught him all those years ago, experiencing a pang from memories as he did so. Exhaling deeply, he closed his eyes. Instead of his mantra, though, more memories resurfaced, as if brought on by the physical positioning of his body. *Him and Aran meditating with the other children...well, if you could call opening their eyes and making faces at each other while the monks had their eyes closed, meditation. The monks playing soccer with them and teaching them their own form of Muay Thai after he and Aran had finished the afternoon meditation...*the images were endless.

A sudden pressure on his hand made him jump. He opened his eyes and looked down. Ryu had taken his hand and was holding it, his palm against Nat's. Ryu's eyes remained closed and he seemed deep in meditation in spite of the small conscious act.

Nat stared at him a moment, before the gentle energy seeped into him where their hands were joined. Ryu's breath rose and fell gently, and his lips were slightly parted. The gesture seemed strange, out of place for what they were doing, but the feeling of Ryu's hand over his was sweet and made Nat wish they could simply sit there like that without ever needing to do anything else.

This time, when he closed his eyes, the memories ebbed away, leaving a quiet darkness. It had been a long time since he'd experienced such quiet. Any sense of inner contentment he'd known had eluded him since Aran died.

He didn't know how much time had passed before Ryu squeezed his hand again. Opening his eyes, he turned and found Ryu's innocent gaze on him.

"I need to call Kiku and tell him I'm all right. He'll be worried."

Ryu felt suddenly, painfully shy. He never meditated in the same room with anyone except Kiku and now...

Without a word, Nat slipped his hand away and went for his cell phone. He flipped it open and dialled before handing it to Ryu.

"Thanks." Ryu accepted the phone and found his heart had sped up a bit. For sure, Kiku would know immediately what had happened between him and Nat and couldn't help feeling he'd been unfaithful.

"I'll wait outside for you." Nat grabbed his T-shirt and sandals and left.

Ryu nodded just as the other end clicked.

"*Moshi moshi*. Ryu, is that you?"

"It's me. Hi."

"You sound better, thank God."

He nodded even though Kiku couldn't see him. "I am. Nat helped me. He did what you told him to do."

On the other end, Kiku exhaled, obvious relief. "I sensed that he would. He felt terrible. I've been worried."

"That's why I called. So you'd know I'm fine. I...miss you." This was the time of day they sat down to supper together, he and Kiku and the others. Being without them was like being without his wonderful close family. And he was close with them, in spite of the difficulties of living together. Even with Yuzo.

"I miss you too. Very much."

A strange feeling tickled Ryu's insides. Something in Kiku's voice… "How are you doing?"

"Okay, considering. I'm just relieved that Agent Phoenix took care of you."

Ryu's gut jumped. "He…did."

"Was he…gentle?"

Gentle. That was his and Kiku's code word for the men Kiku had approved Ryu to care for at the White Tiger. This was also Kiku's way of saying he knew what had happened. All of it.

"Yes. Are you mad at me?"

"Mad at you? Ryu, are you kidding? For what possible reason?"

Relief shivered down Ryu's arms, into his hands, right to the tips of his fingers. "You know."

"Hell no, I'm not mad. If anyone deserves goodness, it's you."

Ryu sighed. Now he didn't know whether to be relieved or disappointed. Had he wanted Kiku to get jealous? "Thank you."

"Hey, Ryu! We miss you!" a chorus of voices erupted in the background.

Kiku laughed. "Everyone misses you."

A pang gripped his chest. "I miss them too. Tell them."

"I will." Kiku paused again. "Ryu, *ai shiite imasu.* Always know that."

Ryu blinked back sudden hot tears. "I love you too."

"I'd better let you go. I think Agent Phoenix is waiting for you."

"He is. I'll call you tomorrow."

"Not if I call you first."

Ryu smiled even though he felt an ache in his chest. Since he was ten years old, he'd always thrived on hearing things like that from Kiku. "Okay. And please tell Yuzo not to run out of green onions for the guests' soup. He always does."

Kiku chuckled, though the sound was sad. "I will."

"Bye." Ryu waited until Kiku had clicked off completely before pressing the 'end call' button. Something about Kiku's voice nagged at him. There was something his friend wasn't telling him, he just sensed it. The uneasy feeling stayed with him as he slipped on his sandals and went outside.

Nat was standing in the walkway next to that Tongmee guy. Nat's white T-shirt stretched across his back muscles. He turned just as Ryu clicked the door to their room shut. "Everything okay?"

Ryu's gaze darted to Tongmee and back. Something about that guy reminded him of some of the yaks he'd grown up around. Cold-hearted. Looking at Nat, however, again brought a feeling of relief and safety, so he nodded. "Fine."

A look flashed through Nat's large eyes that conveyed doubt, but he didn't comment. "Do you mind walking? It's only a few blocks to the place we're going."

"No." Though he wondered how he was going to be able to relax with Tongmee sitting there, emanating a distinct sense of dislike.

"Cool. Let's go. See you later, Tongmee."

"See you."

Ryu fell into step with Nat. "He's not coming with us?" he asked when they'd emerged from the covered walkway to the dirt drive.

"No. I thought it best he stay back with one other guy and watch over the room."

"Oh." He couldn't help a grin. Just being out of Tongmee's presence made him feel lighter.

To his surprise, the corners of Nat's full lips turned up. "I thought you'd be glad. Me too."

"Aren't there three other people?"

"Yeah. You won't see them, though, unless I point them out to you. To give you a sense of privacy."

"Okay." That sounded fine to him.

After several minutes, Nat led him around a corner onto a busier street. The place was touristy with palm trees, lots of signs, cafés and souvenir shops, and the atmosphere was both relaxed and festive. Not so different than Ni-Chome, especially when Ryu saw how many gay couples were walking around.

"The beach is very close by. I'll show it to you after we eat. Do you like *pad thai*?"

He chuckled. "Sure. I grew up on it. My mom makes some of the best."

"Well, this is the best in Phuket." Nat stopped by a place that didn't have a door and gestured. "After you."

Ryu went in, aware of Nat close behind him.

"Nat! Hey!" A high voice echoed through the small place and several people looked up.

A woman was weaving her way through the maze of low tables in the crowded place, waving her arms. Her long black hair swung in a ponytail with each step. "Nat! You sexy guy!"

Ryu turned and saw Nat's cheeks darken as he stepped forward. The woman grabbed him up in a hug. She was nearly as tall as he was and gripped him tight.

"You've been gone too long, honey!"

"Hey, Deena."

Damn. She was probably a girlfriend or something like that. Nat was so hot, no doubt he had anyone he wanted.

Nat pulled away and gestured to Ryu. "It's good to see you. I have a friend with me. This is Ryu. Ryu, Deena. Don't let her intimidate you."

Deena swatted at his arm. "Nat, you're still bad." But she was smiling and turned to Ryu. "It's nice to meet you." She winked.

"You too." She seemed friendly enough, though Ryu hated the distinct jealous feeling that now scratched at his gut.

"I'm training Ryu."

Deena's eyebrows rose. "Oh! So that's what they call it these days. I don't know who to be more jealous of. Anyway, come sit down." She picked up Ryu's hand and led them to an empty table in the corner. "Make yourselves comfortable. Nat, are you going to stay around a while this time?" she asked as they settled against the colourful triangle cushions.

"Yeah, a while."

"Good. Because you've been away too long." She gestured to a young boy who ran over and poured glasses of water. "Do you want the usual?"

Nat nodded. "Make it two. And make it good."

"You know I always do." Deena winked and hurried away.

Nat chuckled. "Deena is outspoken. Always has been. We've known each other since we were five."

"She seems to...like you." Ryu sat back, as if movement could displace the discomfort in his gut.

For a second Nat looked puzzled. Then understanding lit his face. "No, not really. Not like that. It's just that I remind her of Aran. Even when we were kids, she used to say she wanted to marry him one day."

"Oh."

"Yeah. The three of us were inseparable and used to spar together."

Ryu frowned. "Spar? But she's a girl."

Nat laughed again. "Next time she comes over, take a closer look."

After a moment, Ryu saw Deena emerge from the back, balancing a tray with two tall glasses. She came towards them. "Thai iced tea on the house." She set a glass in front of Ryu. Her manicured nails were bright red and her arm was slender, feminine. Her breasts pressed against her T-shirt and her legs were slim and smooth, leading up to a round bottom. He looked at her face again. Deena was pretty but there was something about her he couldn't name. Something...different. "Thank you," he said, for the tea.

She winked at him again. "You're welcome, honey. Nat, where did you find such a cute friend?"

Nat grinned at her. "Luck."

She made a face and set a glass in front of him. "Why can't I have luck like you?"

"What's wrong with Marco?"

"Nothing. He's a sweetheart. We're happy. Five years now!" She wiggled the fingers of one hand, showing off a gold band. "He's just not a fine fox like you two."

Ryu felt his cheeks burn.

"You're embarrassing my friend, Deena. Leave him alone or no tip for you."

"I don't want a tip, honey. I prefer the whole thing, or nothing." She laughed and patted Nat's shoulder. "I'm so happy to see you."

"You too."

When Deena was gone again Nat smiled at him. "Well, did you figure it out?"

He shook his head. "Something's different about her, but no. I didn't."

"She's a *kathoey*."

Ryu's eyebrows went up and his eyes were wide. Damn, that innocent look sure sent warm ripples through Nat's chest.

"*She* is?" He grinned. "I've never met anyone like that before."

Nat laughed. "Would you have known?"

Ryu's laughter blended with his. "I guess not. Is she…all the way changed?"

"I'm not sure. She started the whole process when we were fifteen. And even though she's outspoken, as you've noticed, she doesn't discuss the details. Only her husband knows for sure."

At that, Ryu's expression looked distinctly relieved. "I thought maybe you and she were…you know."

That's when Nat realised what was going on. Ryu had felt jealous. Damn, he couldn't help feeling flattered. "No. Never. We were always just friends." He almost said he would have felt funny about being with her when she was in love with Aran, and stopped at the last second. That would have been really stupid considering Ryu's story. He'd already done enough stupid things with Ryu in one day…

Ryu nodded. "I see."

In moments, Deena was back with two steaming plates of *pad thai*. Nat squeezed some lime over his food and picked up his chopsticks. "Enjoy."

"Thanks." Ryu held the bowl close to his chin and picked up a mouthful with his chopsticks.

Nat did the same only stopped in mid-movement, unintentionally captured by Ryu's lips as he pushed his food past them. After another moment, he forced his attention back on his own meal so he wouldn't make Ryu feel like a piece of meat again, the way he had earlier, and concentrated on giving Ryu a nice evening. If anyone needed to have some enjoyment, it seemed that Ryu did. Being in hiding made stress reduction even more important. For both of them. Though he wasn't sure the kind of relaxation they'd had earlier should happen again.

When they were finished, Deena came back. "How about some fried bananas?"

Ryu looked shy. "No thank you."

"Not for me either, Deena. I'm stuffed."

"Hey, I'm the one trying to keep the girlish figure here." She smiled then leaned down closer. "It's on the house."

Nat put a hand on her arm. "Are you sure?" She didn't own the place and he didn't want to get her in trouble.

Deena winked. "No problem. It's not every day Nat Phoenix the 'Thai giant' comes into this place."

Nat's cheeks burned at the mention of his popular nickname. "Okay. Thank you."

"No problem. Hey, you and Ryu must come to my house tomorrow night. Big party. No special occasion. Just because. Although, your coming for a visit is reason enough to celebrate." She looked at Ryu. "He and his brother were my best friends in the world."

Ryu smiled at her, a soft look that made Nat's insides feel all mushy.

Deena returned the smile then looked at Nat. "Will you come?"

"Can I let you know tomorrow?"

"Sure. In the meantime, Nat, you show this cutie pie a good time. He needs to relax." She picked up their plates and rushed off.

Ryu's eyes went wide again. "What did she mean?"

Nat chuckled. "Don't be alarmed. Deena is highly observant, more than the average person. She prides herself on her feminine intuition and probably picked up on your tension. She would have been a good detective. She just preferred to *date* cops rather than become one."

Ryu's brow remained furrowed. "Do I look that...unrelaxed?"

Again, Nat held himself back from saying something stupid, such as how worried Ryu had looked after his phone call and how that worried look hadn't left his face all through supper.

Nat squelched the urge to reach across the table and touch Ryu's cheek. His other two agents were at a nearby table and the memory of Tongmee's terrible eavesdropping was too fresh. "Don't worry about it. Let's go for a walk on the beach." The sooner they were in a quieter place, the sooner he could question Ryu about that phone call.

Chapter Six

A balmy breeze ruffled Ryu's shorter hair, and the gentle swells of the surf breaking on the shore was the only noise. The music and café sounds of Phuket had faded into the background as they walked farther down the beach. If Nat hadn't known better, he'd have thought that they were on a romantic moonlit walk. With Agents Seinalloy and Chuek less than a shout away, this was not exactly a romantic date. Even though he wished it were.

Ryu stopped suddenly and bent over. When he straightened, he was holding a shell. "I thought I felt something hit my toe." He stood quietly then, running a fingertip over the smooth surface.

Nat watched Ryu touching the shell as if it were the most delicate piece of porcelain. A shiver passed over his skin. He hadn't expected the sudden wish that *he* were the shell in Ryu's hand. He cleared his throat. Time to speak about the phone call. "Ryu, what happened in your conversation with Fujimara? You've been tense ever since." Nat's stomach tensed as he asked the question and saw Ryu's shoulders stiffen as well.

Ryu stopped and turned to him. Silvery moonlight cast an alluring glow on his soft features. "Nothing, really. I swear. It was just...a feeling I had. Like he wasn't telling me something."

"Maybe it's just the stress you're all under."

Ryu shook his head. "No. I've known him for seventeen years. This was a new feeling. Kiku's always been honest with me."

Nat raked a hand through his hair. Seventeen years was a long time. Hard to believe that Fujimara was *always* honest with Ryu. "I need to find out."

"Please, don't! I don't want to know." Ryu's hand landed on his arm. Warmth snaked through Nat's biceps at the touch and his hand froze on the cell phone clip. He sighed. It was already getting too damn difficult to say no to Ryu. But in this case, he had to. "I'm sorry." He flipped open the phone, dialled, and requested a translator when Fujimara answered.

"Fujimara, I need to be kept current of everything that's going on. Ryu is worried you're not telling him something."

A pause for the translation followed. "Ryu is right," Fujimara answered. "I'm going to see Taro Suzuki's father and Ryu's father tomorrow. I plan to tell them the truth...what Suzuki did to the man's son. I'm going to beg for their help."

"Are you sure that's wise?" Nat glanced at Ryu who was staring at the phone in his hand.

"No. I don't know anything. But I've withheld the truth all these years and the situation has only worsened. The truth must come out, and I pray it will help."

"You realise you can't keep this from Ryu. He must know also." Nat's heart sped up as the implications for Ryu sank in. The poor guy. He probably didn't want to hear his father's response. Or lack of response, after what he'd said before about his father punishing him if he knew about the rape. All Nat wanted to do in that moment was take Ryu in his arms and kiss the problems away.

"I know. I had wanted to wait and see how Naboru Miyazaki responded. If he doesn't get angry for his son, then I don't want to break Ryu's heart again with such news."

Nat heaved a deep sigh. "It will only be worse if you lie." He didn't possess any desire to break Ryu's heart either. "Please let us know tomorrow what happens."

"You have my word."

Nat ended the call and clipped his phone back on. Damn. "Come on, let's walk a bit more."

"What happened?"

Damn again. "Fujimara is going to see Suzuki's father and your father tomorrow." He walked a few more steps then suddenly realised Ryu wasn't with him. He turned just in time to see Ryu drop to his knees in the sand. "Ryu!" He dashed over and dropped next to him. On instinct, he put an arm across the other man's shoulders and pulled him close. "It's all right."

But Ryu's upper body was trembling. Nat could feel the tremors against his inner arm. Ryu slumped forward, his head in his hands, fingers curled into his hair, in the position Nat was quickly coming to recognise as a posture of extreme frustration and anxiety.

From a short distance away, Nat saw his other agents step forward to offer assistance, but he waved them off. From what he knew of Ryu so far, too many people crowding him would make things worse. "It's all right, Ryu." He said it over and over. There had to be something more effective to say, but his tongue felt frozen. All he could do was squeeze Ryu's shoulder and give him someone to lean on.

For what seemed a long time, Ryu sat that way, his fingers moving against his scalp. The way he did it gave Nat a funny feeling he was copying someone else who did this. Fujimara, perhaps. Suddenly, he looked up. To Nat's surprise, his eyes were dry, but incredibly, deeply sad. "Kiku is cracking."

Nat stared at him. Unwittingly, his gaze fell on Ryu's soft lips. "What?"

"He's cracking. From this pressure. You don't understand, Nat. He's never hidden anything from me. I know that sounds impossible, but it's true. Oh God." Ryu moaned and hugged his legs, knees bent. "This is awful. I have to go back. I have to be there."

"He'll be all right, Ryu."

Ryu sighed. Moments passed. "I suppose so. He was always tough. But then he changed. As if..." His shoulders sagged and he shook his head.

Nat didn't push him to finish the sentence. He sat quietly, letting his hand still rest on Ryu's shoulder.

After a minute Ryu looked up again. This time, the moonlight made his eyes look misted over. "I *don't* want to know what my father will say to him."

Nat understood. Fujimara had voiced it. Ryu's father might not be upset at all for his son's pain. He squeezed Ryu's shoulder again and then let his touch slide across Ryu's upper back. "I'm sorry this is so hard. Would you listen if I tell you the right thing to do in this moment?"

Wordlessly, Ryu nodded.

"Get some rest. It's been a hell of a long day and you need to rest." He cupped the back of Ryu's neck and brushed his thumb back and forth on the skin. Another moment and Nat slipped his hand away to stand up. "Come on." He held a hand out.

The other man heaved a deep sigh. For a moment it looked like he might refuse, but then he took Nat's hand and pulled, levering himself to his feet.

Without thinking, Nat draped his arm across Ryu's shoulders again as he led him back down the beach. As it had before, Ryu's body fit perfectly against him, even as they walked and Nat couldn't help the protective...no, possessive feeling that surged in him. If he wasn't mistaken, it seemed that Ryu liked it too, pressing into him with each step.

Agent Chuek approached him as they came off the beach. "Everything all right, Phoenix?"

"Yes, thank you. He needs to rest. Difficult times."

Chuek nodded and stepped into place on Ryu's other side. They walked with Ryu between them the rest of the way back to Lew's.

When they got back into the room, the rollaway cot stood in the centre of the floor, still folded up. Nat closed the door and went over to it, noticing that Ryu was staring at it with a kind of crestfallen look.

"Are you going to stay in that?" Ryu perched on the edge of the bed, his hands folded on his lap.

Nat paused, his hands on the ties. "I was."

"Oh." Ryu's look made him feel he'd just said the wrong thing.

"I mean, I thought...I don't know...some people need space for sleeping." Now he felt like a babbling idiot, but again, his tongue wasn't working.

Ryu stood up. "I don't. Need space, that is. It just doesn't make sense for you to use that little cot when the bed is big enough. Don't you think?"

That's when Nat heard the plea in Ryu's voice. Ryu was all but begging Nat to sleep with him. It felt good to be wanted so much but also painful. Ryu shouldn't have had to beg *anyone.* "You're right. It's big enough. Silly to take up more space with this thing." He rolled the cot against the far wall, which wasn't really far considering the room was barely bigger than a phone booth.

The action was rewarded with some light coming back into Ryu's eyes. Just as quickly, though, it faded again. "I'm sorry, Nat. I didn't think. Maybe you're married or something and you feel…weird. You know…about this." He gestured between the two of them.

Nat started. "Married? No. Almost, once, during my boxing career. But I couldn't do it. It wouldn't have been fair to her." That had been a painful experience, letting Rawee down that way. She'd really cared about him. Well, he'd cared enough about her not to deceive her. He went over to his bag to pull out his toothbrush. When Ryu didn't answer, he turned around. "What?"

Strangely, the other man was grinning. "You're sure different."

Ryu's amused expression made him feel weird, like he was on a stage, naked, or something. "What do you mean?"

Ryu shrugged. "Well, half the guys who come to stay at the White Tiger are married."

"They are?"

"Sure. In Japan, most wives don't care. As long as their husband brings home a paycheque and takes care of them and their kids, they mostly don't care if he wants to have sex with a man sometimes." Ryu turned down the covers and then lifted off his tunic.

A strange energy rippled down Nat's arms. Is that what Ryu did all day? Had sex with these men he was talking about? He cleared his throat. That itch of curiosity was back, in full force. "Yeah, I've been wanting to ask you about that place, but now's not the time."

"Why not?"

"Well, we were going to sleep, remember?"

"I'm not too tired to satisfy your curiosity."

Strange, Ryu's whole demeanour had changed, as if they'd entered a territory that was his, a place where he felt confident. A memory of that afternoon resurged, of the way Ryu had kissed him, so passionately, yet so expertly, as if he'd been trained to milk pleasure from a man's lips. God, he was so strange…so…fascinating. Nat felt pulled to him like a moth to light…yet what happened to a moth on a burning hot light? "It's not a…a brothel, right?"

Ryu winced visibly. "No. I mean, the technical definition of a brothel is you go in and pay to have sex, then you leave, right?"

"I guess so."

Ryu toed off his sandals then pulled the tie on his pants and slipped them off. His sloping lean muscles flexed with each movement and the colours on his skin made Nat's mouth water again. "Not everyone who comes to stay comes for sex," he went on. He folded his pants,set them neatly back in his bag, then perched on the edge of the bed again, hands at his sides, giving Nat a perfect view of that pouch in front again. "These guys work like fiends all week, making money, pleasing their families. Complete stress. So for a little while, they come to relax, get a massage, go to the baths, have a young man fuss over them, pamper them. Then they can go out and face their crappy lives again."

Nat stared at him, struck by the sense of purpose in Ryu's voice. He thought at first this was some kind of rehearsed speech. But it didn't seem to be.

"Once in a while, though," Ryu went on, "someone comes for instruction in the White Tiger path."

"Instruction?"

"Yeah. To find enlightenment."

"Through…sex." Nat felt the heat of the topic ripple right down to the head of his cock.

Ryu nodded. "Through the correct use of life force." He sighed, making the white tigers across his hard chest move. "I guess if you want to call it a brothel, you could." His gaze, strangely, was still innocent, though Nat wondered how the hell *that* was possible with a guy who probably gave blowjobs and who knew what else, all day long. When had he had time to train as a boxer?

Nat cleared his throat. "Have you…um…found enlightenment…that way?"

The other man shrugged. "I don't think so. Not yet. But it's my own fault. I don't have a partner, so I don't practice enough." Sadness settled into his brown eyes again.

"You don't?" That itch of curiosity was now maddening and Nat found himself closing the small distance between them. "Of course, I want to ask why, but it's none of my damn business."

"You can ask, Nat. It's because I haven't wanted one." He raised a sad gaze. "How could I have Kiku pair me off with some guy when I wanted to practice with *him*?"

Nat's heart squeezed and he sank down on the bed next to Ryu. Whether Ryu meant to or not, he seemed to have a gift for rousing Nat's sympathy. "Sorry."

Ryu shrugged. "It's not your fault. But…" He paused. A shy, about to make a confession look flashed across his face. "I…used to wish sometimes that *you'd* come in to the White Tiger. I would have wanted to partner with you."

A shiver passed over all his nerve endings. "With me?"

Ryu looked at him as if he'd asked the dumbest question possible. "Yeah, with you." His softly rounded cheeks coloured. "I've had a million fantasies about you since the first time I ever saw you fight on ESPN."

Damn, that had to be more than seven years ago, when he'd been at that last bit of clawing and fighting to the top of the WBA rankings. Now he felt his own cheeks burn. He'd never considered himself as sexual fantasy material. "Ryu, I don't know what to say."

Ryu's eyes had a pleading, sheepish look. "Please, tell me that's not ridiculous because I feel so completely exposed."

Nat closed a hand on Ryu's shoulder. The inked muscle was deliciously warm and hard to his touch. "It's not ridiculous. That's the nicest thing anyone's ever said to me. Thank you." Indeed, it was. Especially from Ryu. He seemed to have some kind of measuring system with Fujimara as the ideal. He sort of hoped to meet this guy Ryu worshiped. At least to find out what ideas about physical beauty Ryu carried around in his mind.

Ryu stared back up at him. His lids dropped slightly, in a sensual way and he tilted his face up, just a bit.

Warm shivers travelled through Nat's body, through his nipples, down to the tip of his cock, which was tight and pushing now at his trousers.

"I swear I'm not trying to seduce you," Ryu whispered.

Nat brushed his thumb back and forth on Ryu's shoulder. "I should never have said that. It doesn't matter if you are." He leaned in closer, close enough to feel Ryu's breath pulse over his lips. "It's…incredibly flattering."

Ryu's face dipped down. "Come on, you must have offers all the time."

Nat looked at him, silent for a few seconds. Ironic that a guy who did what Ryu did for a living would be worried about something like that. "Some offers. But not with quite the…appreciation in them." He let out a breath. Finding the right words was quite a chore with this guy.

At that Ryu looked up. Surprise replaced the embarrassment. "Really?"

He nodded. "Really."

Ryu furrowed his brow. "I just can't imagine you not being appreciated."

Truthfully, Nat felt the same way about Ryu. It had been quite a surprise that he wasn't hot and heavy with Fujimara. That was still a tough one to believe. Even so, if there *were* other people out there in the world who'd spent more than a decade entertaining sexual fantasies about him, Ryu was the only one he'd met, and he had to admit it was damn flattering. Which reminded him… He reached up and traced the rounded contour of Ryu's cheek. Damn, the guy was so pretty it made him ache.

Ryu pulled in a breath. "This was one of my fantasies," he breathed.

Heat fanned in Nat's belly. He became aware of Ryu's scent, of the way the earthy aroma pervaded him, made his cock get even harder than it already was. Nat was also aware that they were in a capsule of some sort, a contained bit of space and time in which the usual rules of life didn't seem to apply. And he was going to take advantage of it. As long as Ryu was into it too. And he did seem *quite* into it. "Oh yeah?"

Ryu nodded. He seemed to be trembling and inched even closer. "Yeah."

A wild feeling began to break loose in him. He cupped Ryu's cheek, ran his thumb across that sensuous bottom lip. "Is there more to this fantasy?"

Ryu's head moved up and down again, against his hand. "Lots more."

"Show me, please."

"Okay." Ryu leaned in closer and brushed his lips across Nat's.

Nat's breath caught. His eyelids shuttered. Arousal, intense and engulfing, immobilized him.

Kuso! How many guys really got a chance to fulfil a wet dream like this? Ryu closed his eyes, breathed in Nat's male scent. Clean and perfect, no cologne or anything. Just hot man mixed with the salt breeze from the beach.

He cupped one rugged cheek and kissed Nat again. Nat's breath was pumping short and harsh. His lips were parted and Ryu slipped his tongue in, dancing it against Nat's. He tasted so damn good, musk blended with the flavours of what they'd eaten, garlic, peanuts, lime, the tart-sweetness of the tea. Heaven.

Nat's fingers chafed his shoulder, the tight movements conveyed more arousal. He seemed to be holding back, letting Ryu do whatever he wanted.

A million times, Ryu had pictured kissing the other man just like this. Sometimes he imagined Nat was sweaty and panting from fighting and Ryu had just dressed his wounds. Sometimes he'd bathed him and rubbed his hard muscles. But whatever happened first, he always ended up doing this...

Ryu slid off the bed, never breaking their kiss. With his hands on Nat's shoulders, he centred himself between those powerful thighs and dropped lower, so he could kiss Nat everywhere once he left his mouth.

Neck and throat, over his Adam's apple, the skin salty and tangy. Nat's large hands rested on his upper back, tension coiled in them. Nat broke the kiss and yanked off his T-shirt, then sat, hands resting on the bed, seeming to offer himself silently.

Ryu slid his tongue across Nat's collarbone. The salty-sweet flesh stimulated his taste buds. Sliding his hands down Nat's bulging arms, Ryu continued down the man's broad chest, over to one side where he feasted on one nipple.

Nat groaned. His chest heaved under Ryu's mouth and the small brown disk tightened against his tongue.

Ryu's thoughts melted away as he kissed a path over to the other side of Nat's chest. Nat tasted just as good as he'd always imagined. Better, because this time he was real. All male heat, warm flesh and rock hard muscle. It didn't matter that Nat wasn't in love with him, the way he was in Ryu's fantasies. Even if it never happened again, at least he'd had these moments.

Ryu pulled the tie of Nat's pants and the waistband fell open. He lifted his mouth from Nat's chest so he could look at the man's dragon. Thick, veined, the same burnt-toffee hue as the rest of him, only reddish. Jutting up over a firm sac, full of delicious yang force. Nat was perfect.

Ryu's mouth watered over the flawless shape of the head where a drop of cum glistened. He leaned over and licked it off. Mmm, more salty-sweetness.

Suddenly, Nat's fingers closed in his hair. "Ryu." His voice was thick, hoarse.

"What?" His heart pumped suddenly from fear. "Did I do something wrong?"

"No. I just…can't think…straight. I'm…safe."

Relief. For a second he'd thought Nat wanted him to stop. He nodded. "Me too," he whispered and dipped his face back down to that delicious cock before Nat could speak again.

Ohhhh. He closed his eyes and took the head in, delicately traced the plump lobes with the tip of his tongue. Just the head of Nat's cock filled his mouth, made his own dragon so hard, it felt like it was going to bust the g-string right off him.

Nat groaned again and one large hand settled on Ryu's head, thick fingers laced through his hair.

Ryu tensed for a second. In spite of everything, he didn't want Nat to grab his head and force him deeper. But Nat's hand only rested gently, fingers agitating through his hair. Something about the tiny movement conveyed gratitude, as if he hadn't gotten this in a long time. Hard to imagine.

Tightening his lips a bit, he took Nat's cock in deeper.

"Ryu."

Wow, Nat was whispering his name. Just like in his fantasies. Ryu sucked, a rhythmic pull that made Nat's cock slide against his tongue. Another dragon's tear seeped out and slipped down Ryu's throat. He moaned around the thick member in his mouth. Heaven.

Ryu's mind darkened, emptied in a sweet way as Nat flooded his consciousness. Nat's musky scent. Nat's groans vibrating through the air. Nat's fingers in his hair. His densely muscled thigh under one hand and the thickness of his cock in Ryu's mouth. The taste of velvety skin stretched over that hard stalk.

Ryu pushed down, took Nat's dragon in as far as he could go. Nat moaned and clutched Ryu's hair. Encouraged, he sucked a bit harder and slid back, plunging down again. Nat seemed to like that motion a lot, especially when he pumped the hard shaft between his wet lips in a slow, even tempo, earning a groan and a clutch each time.

Holy Buddha! Nat had never had a blowjob quite like this. Ryu kept a slow, even rhythm, a pressure with his mouth that sent spirals of tingling pleasure deep into Nat's balls, across the tops of his thighs. All he could do was rest his fingers in Ryu's sleek hair, close his eyes and take it.

His breaths, panting at first, had evened, rising and falling with the rhythm of Ryu's sucking. He couldn't even lift his eyelids a fraction, as much as he wanted to see the other man's head bobbing up and down over his cock. The inside of his mind, behind his lids, was dark, quiet, and all he could hear was the gentle suction of the other man's tongue against his shaft. Dark…quiet…except for…

Twinkling lights. As if he was watching the night sky in his head. His body relaxed, unclenched, even though the unbelievable suction on his cock continued. The pleasure fanned out…up his belly, through his ass, down to the tips of his toes and fingers. Unbelievable. He was in heaven.

Somewhere in his consciousness he felt Ryu's fingertips caress his balls while sucking him. The sensation of Ryu's mouth was hot, wet, incredible, as if Ryu lived to do this.

Unbidden, images rose. Scenes from his life. *Him and Aran running on the beach. Sparring. Laughing. Teasing Deena mercilessly, jostling her around between the two of them in the ocean. He could even see the look on Deena's face through the foamy splash of waves.* She pretended to hate the twins' teasing but really couldn't get enough.

Something yanked him back. Ryu was sucking faster, harder. The blinking lights in Nat's mind exploded, like bright stars. He felt the eruption in his cock, but couldn't open his eyes. His hands slipped from Ryu's hair and he sagged back, elbows underneath him on the bed, while his cock emptied itself.

With his eyes still closed, he could hear his own heavy breathing, mingled with Ryu's. Finally he was able to drag up his eyelids and stare.

Ryu's eyes were closed, his torso tilted back, body, neck and face coated with milky cum. His lips were parted and his breathing rose and fell heavily. He seemed to be in another world.

His eyes opened. The dark pupils seemed unfocused, for just a moment, but then he smiled. "Thank you, Nat," said softly.

Nat stared at him. "Thank me?" he breathed. "That was...incredible." He levered himself up and reached for Ryu. "Come here."

Ryu accepted his hand, let himself be tugged to his feet and manoeuvred to the bed.

"Lie down. Let me clean you off." He used gentle pressure to get Ryu to lie down

"You don't need to clean me off, Nat. I'm absorbing your yang. It's potent and wonderful."

Nat chuckled. It was nervous laughter. Ryu made such strange pronouncements. The things he said and the concepts in his mind were so alien. Yet...sweet. "I'm glad you think so." He stepped out of the fisherman pants that pooled around his ankles, grabbed tissues and sat back down next to Ryu, wiping at his skin.

He thought Ryu would protest again, but he lay quietly, letting Nat clean him off.

Ryu's gaze was steady on him and he seemed to enjoy the attention. "I meant thank you for letting me have my fantasy."

Nat swiped the tissue across Ryu's chin. "I'm the one who should be thanking you." He'd never had a blowjob that made him see twinkling lights, or pleasant memories from his life, either, for that matter.

A gleam of satisfaction came into Ryu's eyes. "It relaxed you, I can tell."

Nat grabbed more tissues. Apparently, Ryu was correct about his abundant yang. "Definitely." He sat back to wipe Ryu's chest and got a glance of the other man's erection. The head of his cock had escaped the confines of the pouch and yet Ryu didn't seem inclined to do anything about it. He seemed content to lie there, letting Nat wipe him off.

Nat wiped the last bit away and tossed the tissues in the wastebasket. "Hey, I think it's your turn now."

Ryu frowned. "For what?"

Nat let his hand land on Ryu's thigh and slid it close enough to Ryu's hard cock to make his point. "For that."

Ryu's eyes widened and a strange look flashed across his face, almost a look of…guilt. "Only if you want to."

Nat caressed Ryu's thigh. He stiffened. Maybe Ryu wouldn't like it and this was his delicate way of saying so. After all, Nat wasn't skilled, the way he was. Doubtless if he gave Ryu a blowjob, the other man wouldn't see lights twinkling in his head. He looked down. "If you don't want me to, it's okay." The other man's erection brushed his inner forearm and Ryu sucked in a breath.

To his surprise, Ryu shook his head. "I do want you to."

Relief prickled through him. "For a second, I thought maybe your fantasies didn't include that, or something." No need to air his insecurity about Ryu's expertise.

"My fantasies didn't include that."

Nat's heart thumped. "Really?" *Eesh*.

But then a grin curved Ryu's lips. "Not because I don't want to imagine it. I usually come before I get to that point."

Now he could laugh, and slid his palm over Ryu's cock, fingertips toying with the exposed head.

"Ohhh." Ryu's eyelids fluttered and his hips lifted, pushing his groin against Nat's hand.

The tiny sound went right through Nat. Ryu's breathing grew immediately ragged. Nat leaned over and closed his lips over Ryu's. Their tongues met and Nat could taste the musk of his own cum in their kiss. With their mouths still together, Nat settled alongside Ryu, pushed into him as close as he could.

Ryu's arm came up around him and his fingertips caressed the back of Nat's neck. Nat moaned and sank his upper body onto Ryu's. The smaller man's cock was smooth and hard between his fingertips and Nat pushed down the pouch of the g-string so he could feel everything.

Ryu whimpered at the contact of Nat's fingertips with his balls. His tongue moved feverishly against Nat's each time Nat brushed over the plump sac while his thumb teased the base of Ryu's cock.

Ryu's hand left his neck and closed over his, guiding his hold higher up and making him rub up and down. Up and down, faster and slower, tighter and easier, Ryu let him know each second just how he wanted it.

Damn. Nat did whatever Ryu wanted him to do. This man was so delicious, so sweet and spicy all at the same time, better than a feast.

Once again, their breathing slowed down and Nat's mind softened, like it had before. His and Ryu's breath passed between them, quietly, gently, in an even rhythm with his hand stroking Ryu's cock.

The shaft thickened and pulsed against his palm. Ryu moaned, a sound that vibrated against Nat's lips, followed by the hot gush of cum. Ryu's hand covered his, never letting go until there was nothing left.

Then Ryu stroked his cheek. He seemed reluctant to end their kiss even though he'd come, and lay wilted, underneath Nat.

Fine with him. Nat was content to stay there like that, kissing Ryu, breathing in his woodsy scent mixed with the musk of sex and sweat.

Finally, Ryu broke their kiss and gazed up at him from heavy lids. "Thank you again, Nat."

Nat grinned at him. "Don't worry about it."

To his surprise, Ryu grinned too. Then he started laughing. "Don't worry about it. That's sweet! I like that." He laughed so much that Nat had to join him.

"Don't worry about it," Ryu said again through a spate of giggles. The sound was infectious and beautiful and each time Nat thought he'd stop laughing, it erupted again from deep in his gut.

Finally breathless, Ryu quieted down and looked up at him.

The look in his eyes made Nat's laughter die in his throat. Nat gazed back down at him. There was a pair of eyes he could get lost in. Without thinking, he cupped Ryu's cheek. "It'll be all right, Ryu," he whispered, then kissed him.

Ryu caught him with a hand behind his head and held him, gently but firmly, so that their lips stayed together for several moments. He seemed to be begging for reassurance through their kiss and Nat tried to give it to him with a tender lick across the tip of Ryu's tongue. When Ryu's hand slipped away, Nat broke the kiss but hovered over him, looking into his eyes.

With a caress over Ryu's hair, he sighed and then rolled off him so he could get more tissues. Ryu gave off a lot of yang too, when he came.

Nat didn't know what had made him say everything would be all right. It wasn't all right. And could get worse. In a hurry.

The only thing that was all right…more than all right…was Ryu's sleek body with its beautiful designs swirling and leaping over his wiry muscles. Ryu's innocent gaze was more than all right and the way Ryu fit in his arms was more than all right.

Nat threw away the tissues, turned off the light and climbed back into the bed. Ryu rolled right over and fit their bodies together, like nesting spoons. Closing his eyes, Nat pressed his lips to the back of Ryu's neck and breathed in that scent again, that heavenly scent. The guy fit so perfectly in his arms, he couldn't believe it. And Ryu seemed happy to be held. Those things were more than all right.

There was more. Ryu had a beautiful laugh. Beautiful like the rest of him. In this moment, only those good things mattered.

The other crap, they'd deal with tomorrow, when Fujimara called with his report.

Chapter Seven

Taro Suzuki looked almost nothing like the old man. For some reason, that brought Kiku a small measure of relief as he knelt before Hayao Suzuki. The *oyabun* of the crime family, though hardened, with the eyes of a hawk, lacked the psychotic glaze that his son possessed.

Such lack of resemblance was not the case with Naboru Miyazaki, who knelt on the opposite end of the low tea table. Though Ryu was much more handsome than his father, the resemblance was evident in the shape of their faces and in the rounded quality of their features. The major difference between Ryu and his father was the expression in the eyes. Ryu looked innocent while Naboru-san always gazed out at the world with suspicion.

Ryu. Kiku felt a pang in his chest. The White Tiger was not the same place without his sweet loyal friend there.

"It is many years since you've crossed my threshold, Kikuchiya-san," Hayao Suzuki said. The formalities of bowing and serving tea now completed, the moment Kiku had dreaded and avoided for so long had finally come. Had Suzuki-san been anyone else, they would have been speaking in his office, seated in chairs around his desk. But Hayao Suzuki was old school.

Kiku bowed again, out of respect, but also for a moment to collect himself. His palms sweated where they rested on his thighs. When he straightened, he caught Naboru's gaze on him. Despite his habitual suspicious look, Naboru-san couldn't hide his hurt. Even though he'd never said a word, Kiku knew how betrayed he'd felt over Kiku's leaving the Suzuki-gumi. "Yes, Father. My apologies."

"What brings you here now?"

Kiku's heart thundered in his chest. If he was breaking *this* promise of silence, how much farther would he be willing to go? "I promise I would never have taken your time if it weren't a matter of life and death."

Hayao Suzuki gave a brief nod. "Proceed."

Kiku cleared his throat. "I have come to beg your help. From both of you." He darted a glance at Naboru then looked down again. "I insulted Taro-san recently, but did *yubizume* a second time to appease him. That was what he demanded even though I am no longer in the family. However, instead of letting the matter lie, he has threatened to take Ryu as…a…slave. I have sent Ryu into hiding while I deal with this threat."

At that, Kiku heard a soft catch of breath.

Naboru-san. "What do you mean…slave?" he asked.

Now Kiku lifted his gaze to Ryu's father, surprised at the wide-eyed look. Naboru had never been a man to show emotion, not even when he'd won a fight. "Naboru-san, when Ryu was seventeen, Taro raped him. He and one other man held him down in his bed and violated him. I came in and got them to leave, but not before…the damage had been inflicted. Now, Taro wishes Ryu to be his possession for the same purpose."

Silence like a stone sinking into a lake, filled the room. Kiku looked down, waiting, feeling anger fill the room like a heavy vapour. Naboru's anger. He dared to glance up, to see the twist around Naboru's lips. Then Kiku looked at Taro's father. The old man sat, rock-still. Very little affected him, ever.

"Kiku-san, why didn't you tell me this?" Naboru's eyes showed horror, the most emotion Kiku had ever seen in them. "You and Ryu both lied. All this time I believed he stayed with you because your place was closer to the gym where he would train."

A chill passed down Kiku's arms and he sweated in spite of the summer heat. "Ryu begged me not to tell you. He was terrified you wouldn't believe him. He feared you'd punish him and send him away to school."

A moment passed. Naboru's anger still simmered in the air.

"That is the real reason why Ryu left home and stayed with you?"

Kiku nodded. "*Hai*, Naboru-san." He bowed his head. "I've insulted you and will accept your punishment."

"No." The old man's voice cut in.

Kiku's gaze whipped up.

Hayao Suzuki's eyes had narrowed to slits. He reached for his tea and took a slow sip, obviously considering a response.

Finally, he set the cup down on the table and rested his hand on his thigh. "As far as you are concerned, Kikuchiya-san, you are no longer a member of this family and as such, my son's actions towards you are not my affair."

Kiku's gut lurched.

"However, Naboru-san, my son has insulted you."

Kiku stole a look at him. The old man had believed him.

"Taro's perversity has intended dishonour to you," the old man went on, "and as such, he should be brought to justice. I

112

have sent him to Taiwan this morning on business, but when he returns, I will summon him here to perform *yubizume* in your presence, at which time, the insult will be amended." The old man's hawk-gaze fell on Kiku. "You and Naboru-san have your own history, also which is none of my affair. Whatever my secretary decides to do with you beyond what I've just decreed, is his business. You're dismissed, Kikuchiya-san."

Kiku bowed low, practically scraping his forehead against the table. "*Aurigato*, Suzuki-san." He bowed a second time and then rose to his feet.

"See him out, Naboru."

"*Hai.*"

Naboru's anger and horror swirled around him all the way to the front entrance of Suzuki's home. The former boxer was of the same build as Kiku and still emanated the raw hunger he had as a fighter, barely mellowed even though he was now sixty.

At the door, Kiku slipped into his shoes and waited, expecting the other man to open it and push him out onto the front walk.

But Naboru only stood quietly, looking straight at him, his expression almost completely reverted to suspicion. "Kiku-san, did Taro perform this...unspeakable act on Ryu under my own roof?"

Kiku bowed his head. "Yes." At least Naboru had believed him as well.

"While I sat in another room, eating and laughing?"

"You were not in the house, Naboru-san. I'm certain Taro would never have dared such a thing if you were there." That was true. Suzuki was as much a coward as he was a pervert.

A cloud of anger surged, filled the air like a noxious fume. "I always wondered why Ryu decided so suddenly to follow

113

my path and start to box. He'd always seemed indifferent to it." Naboru paused and cleared his throat. "I should punish you, Kiku-san, for lying to me all these years. For depriving me of my chance at justice. But I cannot. You meant a great deal to me. Too much to cause you any harm."

Kiku bowed. Ryu's father had meant a great deal to him too, but not as much as Ryu, and he couldn't ignore the ache he felt that Naboru's concern was over the insult dealt him rather than the trauma dealt to his son. Kiku sensed that Naboru did feel pained for Ryu, but the emotion was so covered up as to be almost nonexistent, like Taro Suzuki's good qualities. "*Aurigato*, Naboru-san."

"When Taro returns, I will do what I can to offer you protection from him. I cannot promise more than that. I cannot risk starting a war within the family. The old man is not in good health and if something were to happen to him, Taro would stop at nothing to gain power."

Kiku bowed again. He noticed that Naboru-san did not ask him where Ryu was. "Your protection will be gratefully accepted." Unfortunately, even Naboru's protection would not be sufficient to allow Ryu to return to Tokyo. Taro might be held under control for a while, but if his father fell ill and died, he would never stop threatening anyone connected to the White Tiger, especially after being forced to do *yubizume*. Taro's father had said the matter would be settled between Taro and Ryu's father after that, and so Naboru Miyazaki would have no further recourse anyway. Unless he decided to kill the man. And that was doubtful considering Taro was the *oyabun's* son and Naboru was particularly loyal to the old man.

Kiku sighed and stepped through the door being held open for him. He made his way down the front walk, an awful feeling churning in his gut. He hadn't expected much to come of this meeting. The best he could hope for was that the truth would work on Naboru, anger him enough to deal with Taro in such a way that could go undetected by Taro's father.

Before it was too late.

* * * *

"Kiet, help me, please. Don't let me die."

Nat squeezed Aran tighter in his arms, as if his firm grip could hold back Lord Death. "I won't let you die." Aran's body was so hot, it practically burned Nat's skin and Aran's violent shivers rocked them both. "You must fight, Aran. Fight. I beg you."

But Aran just kept shivering and shivering. Nat squeezed him tighter and shut his eyes, praying fervently to Lord Buddha to spare the one person he loved more than anyone else in the world.

Suddenly, Aran's shivering ebbed away. His body grew still. His skin was still hot but he wasn't moving anymore. Nat opened his eyes. He listened for his brother's breath, tried to feel Aran's heartbeat with his hand on Aran's chest. But there was nothing. Only still silence.

"No! No! No!"

"Nat. Nat it's okay!"

"No! No! No!"

A hand on his jaw kept his head from thrashing back and forth. Nat opened his eyes. The light was dim, shadowy, like dawn. The face looking back at him was alive. Alive. *Ryu.*

"Nat, it's okay. You were dreaming." His hand caressed Nat's cheek.

With a deep breath, Nat wilted against the pillow. He felt hot and sweaty even though cold air pumped from the window rattler. He closed his eyes and took more deep breaths, letting the nightmare fade.

Ryu was still in his arms. But that wouldn't last. Nobody stuck around for long after realising the dream came almost every night. Especially when they learned what the dream was about.

"Nat, are you all right?"

The alarm in Ryu's voice made Nat look up.

Ryu was pressed against him. His face hovered over, sleepy but concerned. His fingertips still rested on Nat's damp cheek.

Nat sighed. He didn't want to see that concerned look turn to one of being freaked out, but best that he just get this over with. "I'm all right. This happens almost every night."

"You dream about your brother."

"Yeah." He rubbed his eyes and heaved another deep sigh. "It's always the same thing. He…dies in my arms."

Ryu's fingers still caressed his cheek. "I'm so sorry." He was silent a moment. "Is that what actually happened?" Ryu's eyes studied his.

He nodded, expecting Ryu to work his way out of their embrace, but he pressed closer and moved his hand over Nat's hair.

"Your real name's Kiet? I assumed that was you he was talking to."

"Yeah, that was me. Kiet Surachong."

Ryu brushed a thumb along Nat's jaw. The touch gentle, reassuring. "That's a nice name."

"Thanks." No one had ever wanted to know his real name before. To the world, even to lovers, he was Nat Phoenix, the Thai giant. And people really didn't want their heroic images stripped away. Except maybe…this man?

"After Aran died, I didn't want to be myself anymore. I wanted to create a new person." He found himself wanting to tell Ryu these things. Not even Deena knew how he'd chosen his fight name. Usually a guy took the name of his training camp as his last name, but that hadn't been far away enough from who he was. It would always have reminded him of that moment, that horrible moment when Aran died in his arms. "One day I read this book about myths of other cultures. And in one, there's this bird called the phoenix. It burns and then rises again from the ashes."

"You were in love with him."

Nat stiffened. Actually, this was the observation that made people run. Again, Nat waited for Ryu to roll away and say he'd had enough. Or something like that. It took a few moments before Nat realised the way he'd said the words was actually…kind.

Ryu frowned. "Oh, shit. I said the wrong thing. I'm sorry."

Nat grasped his shoulders. "No. You didn't. It's just, I've been told this more than once, but always at the end of a relationship." Actually, Rawee had been understanding at first, although she'd wanted to cure him of his feelings, thinking up all kinds of ways he could get over them, as if they were a disease. That had really made him feel worse.

Ryu's eyes clouded over. "You mean…"

Nat laughed in spite of himself. "Yeah, that. Gross." That he was a pervert.

A wide grin broke out on Ryu's face. The smile just lit up his face and eyes, like he was an angel or something. "That's not gross." Then his smile faded. "Why wouldn't you have felt that way about him, being so close and all? Especially when he was so beautiful and strong and brave."

All he could do was stare at Ryu. Words wouldn't come. Feelings swirled inside him, tangled together so that the edges of them blurred. Ryu had guessed his secret, the thing he'd never admitted to anyone, not even himself, but which had controlled everything he'd done and felt his whole life.

Ryu's thumb moved against his skin again. "Don't worry, Nat. That's the best thing you have."

Nat slid his hands from the other man's shoulders to his back. The muscles were deliciously hard and warm to his touch. The scent of Ryu's skin swirled in his nostrils, making him feel a bit drunk. And even though there was a mere few inches of space between their bodies, Nat pulled Ryu closer, so close their cocks pressed together. The contact made his body come alive. Alive the way his insides felt right now. "What do you mean?"

Ryu's hand slipped from Nat's hair to the back of his neck and rested there. "I mean, your love. What else matters?"

Nat's gaze locked with his. How was it that Ryu came out with these things? Just like that? It was obvious he meant every word and Nat felt comforted. More than comforted. Though he hated the fact that Ryu made a career of comforting men. He wanted Ryu all to himself. At least in this moment.

He sighed. Well, they did have this moment. That's all anyone ever had. Without thinking he closed the tiny distance between their mouths and sealed their lips together. Ryu's mouth was soft, yielding to every tiny stroke of Nat's tongue or brush of their lips together. The smell of sex and sweat that had clung from the night before, blended with Ryu's scent and the taste of kisses and Ryu's fingertips toyed with Nat's hair.

Nat slipped his arms around Ryu. If he could have pulled Ryu inside him, he would have, the feel and taste of him was so intoxicating. Especially when Ryu pulled Nat completely on top of him and hooked his legs around Nat's hips.

Suddenly, Ryu broke their kiss, panting. "You can pretend," he breathed "if you want, Nat. I don't mind. If it helps you."

"Pretend?" He was breathing heavily now also, from their kiss and his mind blurred.

Ryu nodded. "Pretend I'm him."

A shiver ran down Nat's back. "What?"

"Pretend. Get out all those feelings you've been stuffing down, giving you nightmares."

Prickly heat travelled through his nerve endings as he understood. "I don't know — "

Ryu kissed him, a hot brush of his tongue over Nat's. "It'll help you." His eyes conveyed dark hunger. "Just a second. I have something." He wriggled halfway out from under Nat and reached over the edge of the bed. Nat heard his hand rummaging in a bag and then he came up with a bottle of golden oil. He opened the top and Nat recognised the woodsy scent Ryu always carried with him. He drizzled some in his palm and spread it on Nat's cock.

Nat pulled in a breath. The hot slide of warm oil on his cock immobilized him. Ryu was wild. The gleam in his eyes, the things he'd just said…damn, were releasing something inside him, from a place with no thought, only feelings and deep, deep sensations. Nat stared, glazed, at Ryu's hand on his cock, the dappling of those fingertips along his length. His breathing was fast and ragged. Electricity seemed to sizzle along the entire surface of his skin.

"Let it out, Nat. It'll heal you," Ryu whispered. He lay back and spread his legs. His oiled fingertips went to his own ass and smoothed it over his hole. Nat stared, watched Ryu's index and middle fingers spread the tight little opening and disappear inside.

"Ohhh." Ryu's eyes closed and his head tilted back as he prepared himself. Then they opened. He closed the bottle and tossed it aside. "Pretend I'm him," he whispered and reached for Nat's arms.

The woodsy scent filled the air and Nat's mind went all fuzzy. The part of him that had hidden his feeling for so long fought the tide threatening to break. No, it can't be right.

"It's all right, Nat. Just pretend." Ryu's eyes were glazed over with desire. His lips were swollen from their kiss and his body was both hard and yielding. He tugged Nat closer and jutted his hips upward, making the head of Nat's cock push against his oiled hole.

Nat groaned. He was losing his inner battle. His body obeyed the pressure on his arms and settled between Ryu's legs.

Ryu didn't know what was making him say and do all this. After Kiku, he'd limited his sex to the occasional blowjob to harvest yang or giving a man—one of the select few Kiku deemed safe enough for him—a happy ending to his massage. But now, he was so hot he couldn't think straight. Nat's cock had been rubbing against his and Nat had been kissing him in such an incredible way… that for the first time in years…since that last time with Kiku…he wanted a dragon deep inside his ass.

Not just any dragon.

Nat's. His fantasy guy. Who wasn't just a fantasy anymore. He was real. And he'd loved someone so much it had broken his heart. Made him human.

Nat was hovering over him. The suggestion had seemed to shock him. But…well, judging from the rocking motion of his hips and the rock hard erection nudging Ryu's opening, the idea seemed to be turning him on.

Ryu reached down and held Nat's dragon in place, pushing down so that the head sank in. He pulled in a breath at the tiny pinch. It had been a really long time and he was really tight.

Nat groaned and pushed in deeper.

Ryu clutched his broad shoulders and pulled his legs back. He couldn't believe this was happening...after so long. Couldn't believe he'd actually wanted it again. Craved it. Demanded it. "Nat," he breathed, "this is what you wanted to do all that time, isn't it?"

Nat's large eyes glazed over. The look in them was tender but also wild.

That was the answer. *Yes.*

He brushed a hot kiss across Nat's full parted lips then stared at him from under heavy lids. "Do it," he whispered. "Don't worry about anything." He slid his hands to Nat's hips and pulled.

Nat groaned and slid in deeper.

Ohhh. One more pinch and then hot sparks...through his whole ass, into the cheeks, tingling his balls, all the way up the stalk of his dragon. The intensity made him tremble but he slid his hands over Nat's hard ass and squeezed, pulling him in all the way. "Yes," he whispered as Nat's cock filled him deep inside.

Nat's hard body covered his. The crush of their torsos sandwiched Ryu's cock, rubbing it in the most incredible way with each thrust of Nat's hips.

Nat pulled back and slid in. Ryu squeezed his ass, feeling the muscles flex each time. This was heaven. Nat was amazing. "Nat," he whispered again, "This is what you wanted—"

Nat cut his words off with the firm press of his lips. The passionate way he invaded Ryu's tongue with his took his breath away. Ryu's eyelids fluttered and his whole body felt like it was melting into the other man's. This was how it was supposed to be. How it had been before...with Kiku. He'd never thought it would happen again. Maybe he *had* earned some good karma by servicing the men who came to the White Tiger. How else could he have this great fortune?

The thought passed through his mind, leaving in its wake a soft, velvety darkness. Quiet, with twinkling lights. Nat's lips were still pressed to his, their mouths open and Nat's breath pulsed steadily, mingled with his. Tingling heat suffused Ryu's hands and spread, like a wind through his entire body. Every ounce of tension drained and the ecstasy concentrated in his dragon as Nat's stomach rubbed it, now engulfed him.

"Ryu?"

Nat's lips had pulled away from his and he could hear Nat saying his name but couldn't find the strength to respond.

Then suddenly, he was floating, drifting...

Chapter Eight

He had to get rid of that ladyboy, and fast. The faggy *yakuza* brat was corrupting a good cop and would probably end up giving Phoenix a disease.

Tongmee backed off behind a clump of palm trees, cell phone to his ear, as he waited for Suzuki to answer his call. Finally, he was able to put all his *yakuza* connections as well as his fluency in Japanese to good use. Getting Suzuki's number hadn't been too difficult.

The phone picked up on the third ring. "Who's this?" Taro Suzuki answered.

"Someone who can get you Ryu Miyazaki." No sense in not getting right to the point.

A long pause ensued in which Tongmee could hear people in the background, as if Suzuki were in a busy place like a restaurant. "How did you get my number?"

"A colleague of yours in Bangkok gave it to me."

"How do I know you're not a cop setting me up? I come there to retrieve what you're offering and then get busted."

Tongmee leaned back against a tree trunk. He glanced over his shoulder to make sure he was alone. "I have nothing on you. No reason to bust you. I just happen to know you want Ryu Miyazaki and I can get him to you."

Suzuki paused again and Tongmee could feel the yak's excitement right through the phone line. For some reason, Suzuki had a thing for this Miyazaki guy. Go figure. "How much would it cost me?" he finally asked.

"I don't want money." That was the truth. He just wanted to get the ladyboy away from Phoenix and out of his own sight. "It'll cost you enough in time and airfare to come get him. He's in Phuket. That's where Fujimara arranged to hide him from you."

"Thailand? He was sent to Thailand?"

"Yes. So, do you want him or not? I can arrange to get him to you. All you have to do is come here."

"I'm in Taipei. It'll probably take me the entire day to get down there."

Tongmee's heart began to race. A strange sense of elation made his head feel light, as if he were floating. "When you get to Phuket, take a room at the Royal Hotel. Just call me on this phone when you're there and I'll get him to you."

"You had better not be setting me up."

Tongmee chuckled. Control was such a beautiful thing. This yak probably had so many people who wanted him dead it wasn't funny. "If I set you up, Suzuki, I tell you what, you can shoot me right in the head."

"If you are setting me up, I'll make sure that happens."

Tongmee ended the call and slipped away from his hiding spot to continue his round of the gym building. Though it didn't matter whether he did surveillance or not. Phoenix and the little fag were locked up nice and cozy in their room, fucking like jackrabbits. Again.

Tongmee smiled to himself. He hadn't felt peaceful, satisfied, in so long. But the thought of justice finally gave him a bit of rest.

He glanced at their door as he passed by and nodded a greeting to Seinalloy who stood nearby. Let Phoenix and his pet have their fun for now. It would be over soon enough.

* * * *

Ryu. Ryu.

Nat was still saying his name.

Ryu could feel Nat's muscular body between his thighs and the other man's thick dragon deep inside his tight passage, but he, himself, was so much larger. Everything that existed was absorbed in his consciousness.

So this was what Kiku had told him about. This glorious floating, freedom from the confines of flesh and bone. He felt free. Completely unburdened. And yet...

Ryu? Are you all right?

Nat sounded so worried. Ryu felt a hand caress his hair.

Yank. The emotional pull to come back was strong. He couldn't let Nat worry like this. Nat was a good man and made him feel so good. He had to get back into his body and reassure Nat he was okay...

The sensation of floating stayed with him even as he went back in. He blinked several times. Nat's face hovered over his and the full force of Nat's hard cock in his ass slammed him into full consciousness. "I'm all right," he managed to say. Speech was difficult, as the bliss of freedom still tingled through him.

Nat's hand passed over his hair again. The touch was so gentle, so...caring. "What happened? I thought maybe you were in that trauma again."

He smiled. "No. Not at all. You...you rocked me into bliss."

Nat's eyes widened. "Really?"

He nodded. "Really. I was floating."

Nat shifted on top of him. "Wow. Glad to help." He leaned down and Ryu accepted a delicious kiss, full of Nat's musky taste.

That's when Ryu felt the sticky warmth. He broke the kiss and looked down to see his cum pooled between them. That must have been when he'd spun out of his body. He shifted his hips and squeezed his muscles around Nat's cock, pulling a groan from the other man. He grinned. "I want you to come, Nat." Sliding his hands to Nat's gorgeous ass again, he squeezed and pulled.

"Ryu," he groaned.

That sounded so beautiful. Hearing his name like that. He tilted his head back, lips parted.

The invitation was taken immediately. Ryu loved tasting Nat's lips and tongue. He had the most masculine, delicious flavour. And it felt so good not to worry, not to be so frightened of the hard, tight slide in his backside, so good to be enjoying it and wanting it.

And being so wanted.

In seconds, Nat groaned into his mouth and Ryu felt the gush of Nat's hot yang cloud deep inside him. He too, moaned as Nat's belly rubbed his cock in the throes of his climax. Then he collapsed and Ryu closed his arms around the sweaty muscular body.

Just as Nat's cell phone rang.

Damn. That had to be Fujimara. Nat slipped out of the haven of Ryu's body and rolled over, groping for his phone clip in the pile of clothes that lay there.

"That's Kiku. I know it." Ryu was already sitting up, his eyes wide. The calm ecstasy that had been there before had mostly vanished.

Ryu's change of expression left him mournful as he flipped open the phone. "This is Phoenix. Go ahead, Fujimara."

"It went as I believed it would, for the most part," Fujimara said through the interpreter. "Suzuki's father wants Taro to do *yubizume* as an apology to Ryu's father."

Nat glanced at Ryu. "And what about him?" He didn't want to say the name out loud.

"Ryu's father?"

"Yes."

A pause ensued, in which Nat's heartbeat increased. He found himself hoping that Naboru Miyazaki would be enraged, ready to kill Taro Suzuki. For Ryu's sake.

"He was angry. That Ryu and I had lied to him. He will offer us what protection he can but he's reluctant to do anything that might start a war within the family. The old man is not well." Pause. "That wasn't all you wanted to know, was it, Agent Phoenix?"

Nat gripped the phone harder. His heart now pumped with anger. This beautiful man in the bed with him had been so shit on, it was unbelievable. "No, it wasn't."

"I understand. I too, wanted the man to say he was going to kill Suzuki for hurting his son, but he didn't. I suppose it's possible he was thinking it, but...truthfully, I didn't sense that in him, at least not at the time."

"Can I talk to him?" Ryu's hand landed on his arm and squeezed.

Nat sighed. "Of course. Here's Ryu." He handed him the phone and listened to the exchange in Japanese. He didn't understand a word, but could certainly surmise what was being said in the manner of Ryu's bent head, the hand raking through his cut hair, the frustration in his tone.

"Kiku, with all respect, why did you have to tell him? You knew this would happen, didn't you?"

"I'm sorry, Ryu. But all these years we've kept it hidden and the situation is worse. I should have told him from the start. The truth is always better."

Ryu clutched his hair with his free hand and exhaled, aware of Nat's gaze on him. Somehow, the fact that Nat was so close, helped. He didn't feel quite so…rejected.

What had he been hoping for? For his father to make a sudden turnaround and actually give a shit? And yet, as he sat, rubbing his head in agitation, he realised…shit…after all these years, he *had* been hoping for that. Had never stopped hoping for it. Not for a second. Even in this moment, he had to know for sure. "Kiku, you see deep into people. Was there anything in his heart that seemed like he wanted to defend me?"

Kiku paused and Ryu heard a deep sigh. "Truthfully, Ryu, there was a little bit there, but it was so buried underneath everything else. I pray that it'll work on him as time goes by."

"Ach! He's made of stone. You're the only person he ever cared about and the best he could do was not punish you. Did he even thank you for making sure I didn't become suicidal or run away and get killed, or anything? No." His heart pounded. "Oh, and he cared about fucking my mother. That's the other thing he cared about. He fucked my mother and made me so that he could look like a normal guy or some shit like that and then he could throw me to the dogs!" He felt helpless as tears slipped from his eyes. He turned his back to Nat. The man had already seen him cry enough. If he didn't think Ryu was a baby before, his opinion would certainly change.

But a large hand clasped his shoulder and squeezed. The touch was reassuring, calming, even though pain wrung his chest.

"I'm sorry, Ryu. God, I say that a lot." Kiku sounded miserable.

Ryu released a long breath. "It's not your fault."

"It's not my fault but I've let things get out of hand." He was quiet a moment. "Listen, your father didn't get where he is by being a superficial man. Give him a chance. I sense that he will respond in some way. He *did* offer what protection he could."

Bitterness clenched inside him. "How kind of him."

Kiku exhaled and Ryu sensed him about to change the subject. "How are things with you and Agent Phoenix?"

Heat burned in Ryu's cheeks. "Good."

Pause. "Ryu, you went there, didn't you? To the second level."

"Yes."

"That's incredible. Finally." Kiku sounded as if he would break into tears. At least he cared. He'd always cared. Which was why it was hard to really get angry with him even though he was fucking up as much as he was succeeding.

Ryu found himself smiling. "Thank you. It just feels weird that…"

"That it can happen with someone else besides me."

"Yeah."

"It just means…"

His heart lurched. "Means what?"

"You have a lot of love."

Ryu turned halfway back. Nat's hand still rested on his shoulder. "I guess so."

"No guessing. It's true. You've worked very hard. You're devoted. And now that bears fruit."

Ryu's gut clenched. "How hard do I have to work for him to care about me?" Kiku would know he was talking about his father now.

"My sweet friend, you have no control over such a thing. No one does."

The tears came and Ryu turned his back again to Nat.

"Ryu, I'm going to do what I can to settle this. I promise."

Kiku never broke his promises.

"Okay." Though he couldn't imagine how Kiku could really do anything. There was no doing anything about such evil people like Taro Suzuki. They lived in their own world, mentally and emotionally. "I should go."

"Me too. I love you."

"I love you too." Ryu waited for Kiku to hang up before he shut the phone. He sighed, too embarrassed by the tears slipping down his cheeks to turn around. Hard to believe he'd been so blissful only minutes before. Then his chest clenched again. "I don't get it," he murmured, as much to himself as to Nat whose hand had slipped from his shoulder to his back and rested there, palm down.

"What don't you get, Ryu?"

He heaved a sigh. "How people bother to have kids when they don't give a shit about them. I just don't know why they bother."

Nat lifted his hand from Ryu's back and stroked his hair. It seemed to relax him. "I don't know, either. It sucks. There's a lot of that here too. Everywhere, I guess."

Suddenly Ryu spun around. "When I was a kid, I had this girlfriend, O-Shin. She always looked so sad. Her father was a lawyer and worked twenty hours a day. He was never home. Her mother got addicted to reading *yaoi* and finally checked into a mental hospital. O-Shin was left at home with a housekeeper all the time. She started dressing like a guy and acting like one. The only time she seemed happy was when we were together. Then the housekeeper told her father we were having sex and he took her away." Ryu's eyes reflected the horror he must have felt at the time.

"That's awful."

Ryu nodded. "I hounded him to tell me where he'd taken her, but he wouldn't even speak to me. When I told Kiku about it, he had me take him to where O-Shin's father worked. On the other side of the city. Then he *made* the guy tell me the truth."

"Where was she?"

He looked down and sighed. "He'd stuck her in a boarding school all the way in England." When Ryu looked up again, his beautiful eyes flashed and a muscle in his jaw twitched. "Like I was some sort of freak who shouldn't be touching her. The worst part was, it was a lie. We weren't having sex at all. All I did was kiss her on the lips. She was really hot as a boy." He looked completely mournful now, and Nat guessed that Ryu had really loved the girl.

"That asshole didn't even know her, Nat. He didn't give a shit if she was happy or not. He just cared how it made him look that she might be having sex. Why bother to have a kid?"

Damn, this guy had suffered. In a surge of protectiveness, Nat reached for him. It was a miracle he wasn't a psychopathic maniac like Suzuki after all this. "Maybe some people's role is just to give birth to the person, like a vehicle or something so then later on in your life, you can find the people who really *do* care." The words were out before he could think about them, emanating from some mysterious place inside him, a place that so much wanted to comfort Ryu.

Smaller hands took hold of his arms and Ryu pushed back, his dark gaze trained intensely on Nat. "Do you really believe that's possible?"

Looking back into Ryu's eyes, Nat realised he did believe that. It wasn't possible for a person like Ryu not to have people care about him. "Absolutely."

His certainty was rewarded with a smile and with some of the unhappiness draining from Ryu's face. "I can buy that then," he said. Then a shadow passed over his face. "I just hope that was the case for O-Shin. She was such a sweet girl. I don't think she ever came back to Tokyo."

Nat reached out and cupped Ryu's cheek. "Hey, I think we should get up, have breakfast and do some training. It'll be good for both of us."

"Okay. Do you think we'll go to Deena's party?"

"Oh yeah. I'd forgotten about that. I'll call her during the day and find out who else will be there before I decide. You can't be too careful."

Ryu nodded. "I understand." He pushed back the covers and started to get up. "You want to shower with me? I think we might both fit in there."

Nat chuckled. His body sure liked the sound of the invitation, but there were things to do. Like call Tongmee and the others. "I'd love to but I have some stuff to take care of before we get out of here."

Ryu grinned. "Suit yourself." Then he disappeared into the tiny bathroom, door closed.

The spray of the shower turned on and Nat went for his phone again to call the other agents.

Tongmee. He didn't relish the thought of dealing with the guy, even though Tongmee had agreed to settle down. It had really been a bad call on the part of Naresuan to bring Tongmee onto this assignment at this particular time.

With a sigh, Nat pressed the speed dial for Tongmee's phone, glad that he'd put Seinalloy outside their door for the last few hours. No doubt Seinalloy had heard him and Ryu creaking the bed springs.

Ignoring the warm thrill of that memory, Nat put his attention on speaking with Tongmee and ignoring the naggingly bad feeling the other agent left him with. "How are you doing today, Agent Tongmee?"

"Better, thanks. Much better."

Tongmee sounded calm. Weirdly calm, as if he'd taken medication.

"Good. I'm sorry for what you've been through recently."

"Don't worry, Agent Phoenix. Life has a way of working out. I'll be all right. I've made several rounds already this morning."

Nat glanced at the bathroom door. Unbidden, he imagined Ryu's wiry form all wet and glistening from soap. "Good. We'll be out soon to get breakfast and then start some training."

"All right. Just let me know what's needed."

At that, Tongmee sounded businesslike again. Almost...normal.

Nat breathed a small sigh of relief. "Okay. Just let the others know, all right?"

"Yes, sir."

Nat ended the call and looked at the bathroom door. Damn, there was that itch again. Hoping the invitation to shower was still open, Nat cracked the bathroom door open and peeked in. Steam and a mist of hot water met his skin. He saw a flash of colour, the kissing *samurai* on Ryu's back just before he turned around.

A grin spread across Ryu's face. "Hey, you changed your mind."

Nat hovered for a second. If he went in there, they had a good chance of not making it out of the room at all until well after lunchtime. Oh well. The desire to go in was too strong to resist. "Yeah, I did." He stepped into the steamy hot little cubicle and closed the door. There was that magnetic pull again, the ache in his hands to feel Ryu's smooth skin and wiry muscles. To taste those lips…

Ryu was holding the showerhead on its hose. "Come here," he said, then aimed the shower hose at him. He sprayed it over Nat's back and down his chest, letting the water douse Nat's skin and hair. Then he held it out, spray-down. "Hold this."

Nat accepted the showerhead and watched Ryu wet a cloth with a bar of soap. In the next second, Ryu slapped the wet cloth against Nat's back and was rubbing in tight circles. Immediately, Nat's eyelids shuttered and he tilted his head upward. Damn, Ryu knew how to make a guy feel good in so many ways. "That's great," he murmured through the noise of the shower spray.

He heard Ryu chuckle. "Just enjoy." The cloth moved down his spine, across his lower back, over both ass cheeks and then down his thighs. Nat supported his weight with a hand against the tile wall and peeked down.

Ryu's dark head was right by his left knee where he knelt, giving full attention to Nat's legs. It felt so damn good, as if he were a statue on an altar that Ryu was cleaning…except for a tickle of discomfort in his gut. Ryu probably washed a lot of guys like this.

He sighed. *Screw it, Phoenix. Why do you care?* Had the circumstances been different, Ryu wouldn't have been here at all.

The cloth was making its way back up his body and Ryu rose to his feet, now giving attention to Nat's front. Ryu's eyes almost sparkled and he was smiling. Nat jumped as the warm cloth touched his balls.

"I won't hurt you, Nat." He wiped gently all around, using the perfect amount of pressure. Ryu seemed to know just what he was doing. His expression was tentative. "Is that good?"

He nodded. "Amazing."

Ryu didn't answer. He sloshed the washcloth across Nat's stomach then over his chest and into his armpits, all in slow, careful circles.

The pampering was really nice but Nat's curiosity itched him still. He almost asked Ryu how many guys he'd done this with. *That* was a question better left unasked and unanswered. However, there were some things he could know at least without suffering. "Ryu, let me ask you something."

"Yes?" The cloth paused on the centre of his chest.

"Why Thailand?"

Ryu looked up at him. That sweet gaze made his insides flutter. "You mean why did they send me here?"

"Yeah."

The other man shrugged and slid the cloth up to Nat's shoulder. "I asked Kiku that myself. He said this is where they could make the fastest arrangements." He retrieved the showerhead from Nat's hand and proceeded to rinse him. "There's a police inspector in Tokyo who came to the White

Tiger undercover. He was looking for Yuzo when Yuzo's uncle couldn't find him. That's because Kiku was hiding *him* from Suzuki at the time. Well, it all worked out, and when Kiku told him what was happening, he offered to help us. His father is ambassador to several southeast Asian countries, so he arranged all this."

Nat leaned back and looked at him. That seemed impossible. "Just like that? I mean, Kiku must be trading information on the yaks in return."

But Ryu shook his head. He replaced the showerhead and turned off the spray. Without missing a beat, he unfolded a towel and started drying Nat's back. "I don't think so. Kiku's vowed never to squeal, even though he probably could tell them a lot."

"You mean, the inspector is helping you just like this? Not expecting anything in return?"

Ryu didn't answer for several moments while he rubbed down Nat's legs. Then he straightened and gave a gentle wipe of the towel across Nat's chest. Ryu's dark eyes looked almost as misty as the steamy room. "Well, Yuzo's uncle and the inspector's uncle were lovers for most of their lives. I think the inspector is helping us because of that, out of love for his uncle and gratitude to Yuzo's uncle who took care of *his* uncle after the war when the man was traumatized and couldn't make a living. He's not asking for anything in return. The inspector is…unusual. He's a man of honour. Like Kiku." Then Ryu's gaze changed and he appeared to study Nat. "Hey, you ask that like you don't believe it's possible. Like *you're* not that way too. I bet *you* wouldn't ask for anything in return either."

The words struck him unexpectedly and all he could do was stare at Ryu.

A look of impatience flickered through Ryu's eyes. "Well? Do you expect people to do things for you just because you did something for them? More precisely, take me for example, would you have expected me to...service you... in return for your protection?"

The mere suggestion made a pain in Nat's gut. "Hell no."

Ryu smiled. "Then you proved my point." He wiped the towel across Nat's back.

But Nat couldn't enjoy the attention anymore. The pain of Ryu's question stayed with him, churning his middle and before he knew what he was doing, he grasped Ryu's arms. "Ryu, that's not what you were doing, is it? Having sex with me because I'm protecting you? Because if it is, I want you to stop."

Ryu's beautiful face crumpled and his eyes looked pained. "Of course not." He squared his shoulders but didn't shake Nat's hands off. Suddenly his eyes flashed in a way that Nat had seen only when he'd demanded that Ryu cut his hair. "Listen, Nat, I'd rather get strung up by my balls on one of those palm trees outside than give you sex out of some kind of obligation. Got it?"

A choking feeling pulled at Nat's throat, probably from having jammed his foot very deeply into his mouth. He nodded. "Got it. I'm sorry." He brushed his thumbs on Ryu's arms. "Really, I got it. I said a stupid thing."

Ryu nodded. "You sure did." To Nat's relief though, he smiled again. "It's okay. I forgive you."

Without thinking, Nat stepped towards him. Ryu was still wet, his colourful skin glowing from the mist over his muscles. It seemed that since their first meeting, he couldn't do or say the right thing with Ryu, only make up for his mistakes and stupid words. He wished a kiss could erase all of it. He leaned down and brushed his lips across Ryu's.

When he lifted away, Ryu was gazing at him, a soft but strange look in his eyes.

Before Ryu could speak, Nat took the towel from Ryu's hands and set it aside. He then grabbed another towel, opened it and wrapped it around the smaller man. "My turn to dry you off. Okay?"

Wordlessly, Ryu nodded and stood, quiet, while Nat rubbed him down, trying to copy the skilled way Ryu had dried him. More discomfort curled through Nat's insides, not so much from having said the wrong thing, but from having Ryu think of him as a selfless, honourable person. Well, if Ryu could view making a living out of punching guys' lights out and then escorting royals around on their vacations and shopping excursions, so be it.

When he was finished, he hung the towel up and took Ryu's hand. "Come on, let's get going."

He led Ryu out of the bathroom and released him so they could both get ready. While they dressed, he couldn't help stealing glances at Ryu, surprised to see him put on actual briefs for underwear, rather than his g-string. He followed that with long boxing shorts and a baggy souvenir T-shirt from the training camp that Lew had left for them as a gift along with the cot. The dark coloured shirt went all the way to Ryu's elbows and not one tattoo was visible. Perfect.

When they were all dressed, Nat went to the door. "Ready?"

Ryu shook his head. "Not yet. There's something important I have to do first."

Chapter Nine

Nat stiffened. "What is it?"

He watched Ryu come and stand in front of him, gaze lifted.

"Well, while I was getting dressed, I realised, you're about to train me, like a teacher. I know about *wai kru*." Ryu clasped his hands, palms flat together and bowed his head. "I know what a big deal it is when a teacher takes a student and imparts knowledge of Muay Thai." With that, he dropped to his knees, hands still steepled in front of him and bowed.

Nat's cheeks tingled. If anyone was more unpredictable than Ryu, he hadn't met that person yet. "Thank you, Ryu," he murmured.

Slowly, Ryu lowered his hands and rose. His gaze was so serious, so intense, Nat felt a shiver right through his chest.

"I miss my coach in Tokyo," Ryu went on. "It was really awful when I had to pull out because of Suzuki. I'd just won my last fight. Not by much, but I won. He'd become a good friend. A...mentor. It's no small thing."

Without thinking, Nat reached out and clasped Ryu's shoulder. "I know." He squeezed and gently steered Ryu towards the door. "Come on."

Ryu's gesture of *wai* stayed with Nat through breakfast and the short walk along the beach they took while they digested.

Back at the gym, Nat put Ryu through warm-up stretches and then demonstrated all the kicks, punches and footwork. Ryu reproduced each move flawlessly, giving Nat the impression he'd actually already learned Muay Thai even though he hadn't said so. Of course, since his last fight had been so recent, he *was* already in fighting condition.

"Hey, Phoenix, looks like your new student is ready to spar."

Nat turned at the sound of Tongmee's voice.

The other agent stood a few feet away in the walkway off to the side of the training area. Tongmee was grinning at him.

A shiver passed through him. "I don't think so, Tongmee."

"I feel ready, Nat."

Nat whipped around.

Ryu was standing close by, a strange look on his face. His gaze was trained on Tongmee. An unspoken, crackling kind of challenge simmered in the air between the two men. Nat had seen this kind of thing...and had done it himself...too many times not to recognise it. "You're not ready," he said firmly.

"I feel ready and I'd like to." His almond-shaped eyes hardened and for the first time since they met, Nat saw the fighter in Ryu. "Maybe Agent Tongmee could spar with me. I'm sure I've not had as challenging an opponent ever."

Nat gave Ryu a look that meant to say, "What the hell are you doing?" But Ryu seemed to ignore him.

To Nat's horror, Ryu turned to Tongmee. "What do you say, Agent Tongmee?"

His horror increased at the glitter in Tongmee's eyes. The agent glanced at Nat then back to Ryu. "I say give me five minutes to wrap my hands and gear up." He then turned and went off in the direction of Lew's office.

Nat was glaring down at him, but Ryu didn't care. His blood ran hot through his veins with the electric hum he always got before a fight. Agent Tongmee needed an ass-kicking. And even if he was unable to give it to him, at least he was going to get in a few good shots.

He went over to his gear bag and pulled out his hand wraps, glad that he'd brought his stuff with him from Tokyo. "You don't have to do these for me if you don't want, Nat. I already know how." His heart was pounding, both from fear of angering Nat but also from anticipation of getting a few kicks and punches in on Tongmee, the bastard. Unlike Kiku, he refused to lose his edge, to mistake spirituality for being a pushover. He and Kiku had argued about this point many times and he refused to back down, even though he adored his friend and obeyed his wishes as much as possible.

Nat huffed and went over to him. "Of course I'll do them for you." He was silent a few minutes as he wound the cloth around Ryu's hands.

Ryu studied Nat's face. "Don't be angry at me," he said. "You know, being spiritual doesn't mean letting people spit on you without defending yourself." He looked into Nat's large eyes. "I heard what he said yesterday, even though I was in trauma. He's a cruel person and I don't like his attitude."

Nat tied the wraps with adept swiftness. "He was wrong to say you're crazy, Ryu. But it *is* crazy to fight with him when you haven't trained in Muay Thai."

"But I have." Ryu felt his face burn as he confessed. He didn't want Nat to be angry. "I'm sorry. I didn't tell you that. I didn't want to say it in front of Tongmee. He makes me really uncomfortable."

Nat's eyes were wide. "When did you train in Muay Thai?"

"When I was seventeen. I studied it for two years before I switched to straight boxing."

The other man sighed. "I don't like this, but I understand." He slipped Ryu's gloves on for him. "Listen, I've seen him spar before and he always leads with his right. The closer you can get in and upper cut him, the better off you'll be. Get in close and stay there."

Ryu smiled and nodded. "Thanks. And I'll be careful." He'd already put on a groin protector earlier and now opened his mouth so Nat could slip in the mouth guard.

And none too soon. Tongmee returned, geared up.

The agent carried a boom box and was grinning like a satisfied cat. "Lew even gave us this to use. *Wong plee gong.* Just like a real fight." He set the boom box down by the side of the ring. "Ready?"

Ryu looked straight at him. The glitter in Tongmee's eyes unsettled him a bit, but his years of meditation kicked in at that moment and he felt centred, aware of the fear that truly underlay Tongmee's hostility. Not that it was going to stop him from kicking the guy's ass. "I'm ready." He followed Tongmee up the few steps and between the ropes of the fighting ring and stood, facing him in the centre.

I can't believe I'm letting him do this. Nat climbed between the ropes in a last-minute decision to referee instead of Karl, one of the gym's trainers who'd offered, and asked him instead to man the music recording and the bell. Karl didn't understand the deeper dynamics going on between Ryu and Tongmee.

But he did, which was the only reason he was agreeing to their sparring match in the first place. He understood Ryu's humiliation of the day before, the way Tongmee had treated him with cruelty in a very low moment.

A crowd was beginning to gather around the ring, as the other guests and trainers stopped what they were doing to come over and watch. A sparring match between two fighters of different weight categories had surely sparked their interest.

Nat pulled in a deep breath, still wanting to stop Ryu from doing this as he positioned himself to one side. "All right, you two, I'm giving you two rounds of three minutes each. No arguments."

Ryu nodded and Tongmee, though seeming to want to argue, nodded as well. Tongmee stared at Ryu from his taller height, a glitter of challenge in his eyes, but Ryu returned his stare, an iron determination on his beautiful face.

Nat's stomach clenched but he looked over at Karl with a signal to ring the bell, then backed off. "All right, begin."

Karl rang the bell and started the *wong plee gong*.

Ryu touched his gloves to Tongmee's in a show of sportsmanship and settled into the fight stance, as did Tongmee. The musical accompaniment of cymbals, drum and Javanese oboe began slowly, sinuously and Nat watched both men begin to rock rhythmically, fists raised, eyes trained on each other.

Tongmee struck first. A straight punch that grazed Ryu's jaw. Ryu danced back, avoiding most of the impact, but he would have a time of it avoiding further offences from Tongmee who had a much longer reach.

Nat saw a tiny grin on Tongmee's lips. A mistake, thinking that your opponent was so beatable that you didn't have to concentrate completely. The taller man's fist came out in another straight punch.

Ryu swerved and regained his balance. His gaze obviously noted that Tongmee led with his right, so the next time Tongmee reached for him, Ryu got Tongmee in the ribcage with a half-shin, half-knee kick.

Tongmee grunted and staggered slightly back. The crowd watching cheered.

Go Ryu, Nat thought as he moved out of their way. Ryu's kick had angered Tongmee, shocking him out of complacence and he moved in with a stronger offence.

The tempo of the music increased. Ryu and Tongmee's kicks and punches increased along with it.

Tongmee moved in closer. He swung with his right. Ryu ducked, stepped into him and got him with a one-two uppercut, first to Tongmee's sternum then to his jaw. Tongmee hit the ropes then bounced back and staggered a few steps before regaining the music's rhythm. For a few seconds, his movements showed he was almost as dazed as he was angered.

Nat glanced at Ryu. The smaller man was guarding his face, never breaking the tempo of the *wong plee gong*. His determination was palpable as he waited for Tongmee's next offence.

Tongmee moved in a bit closer. He feinted then got Ryu on the side of the neck with a round kick.

Ryu went down on one knee. The crowd hissed, seeming naturally to root for Ryu, the smaller, lighter man of the two. Nat had to squelch the impulse to pull Ryu up. All he could do was guard and make sure Tongmee didn't go at him while he was down. In two seconds, Ryu had recovered his feet and resumed his rocking.

The music grew faster. The first round was nearly over. This time, Ryu moved in, getting in a round kick to Tongmee's left inner thigh. Tongmee began to stumble back, but not before Ryu got in a firm straight punch. The impact didn't take Tongmee out, but did keep him back until the bell rang.

Nat looked at Ryu. Ryu was breathing heavily and shaking out his arms and legs. His cheeks, jaw and upper body were reddish from the impact of Tongmee's gloves and kicks, but the determination hadn't left his eyes.

After a small rest, Nat signalled for the second round. Again, Ryu and Tongmee touched their gloves together and began their footwork to the music's rhythm. The tempo was much faster now than in the beginning, urging both Ryu and Tongmee to fight harder.

Several times the two men clinched together, kneeing each other's ribcages and delivering close punches until Nat pulled them apart. Once more, Tongmee delivered a high kick that made Ryu stumble back and almost hit the ground, but he recovered himself and managed to get some more uppercuts into Tongmee's sternum and chin.

The bell rang and the fight was over. Both Ryu and Tongmee had small cuts above their eye as well as vicious red marks from punches and kicks. They were glaring at each other but still touched their gloves together.

Nat put a hand on Ryu's shoulder, relieved as hell that the fight was over. Ryu had held his own quite well, but Tongmee was older and more experienced. "Are you all right?"

Ryu nodded as he pulled off a glove to accept a bottle of water from someone standing on the sidelines. The men around the ring were cheering Ryu as if he'd won even though when Lew added up their points, their scores were nearly even, Tongmee the winner.

Chuek was seeing to Tongmee so Nat tugged Ryu out of the ring and ushered him down the corridor, towards their room. "You fight really well, Ryu," he said, keeping a possessive hand on Ryu's shoulder.

Ryu looked at him, eyes wide. Sweat glistened on his face and around the swelling and redness. "Really?"

"Yes, really. Impressive the way you held your ground with a larger, heavier man."

Ryu bowed his head. "Thank you. I just wanted him to know that I'd defend myself. I'm not a doormat."

Nat squeezed his shoulder before letting him go and holding open their door. "I'm aware of that."

Once inside, Ryu stripped off his clothes immediately. "I'm going to shower."

Nat's cheeks heated and he tried to avoid staring at Ryu's naked body all gleaming sweaty colourful muscles. "Again? You sure shower a lot." This was Ryu's third shower in less than twenty-four hours.

Ryu grinned. "I'm half-Japanese. There's a lot of clean freak in my blood."

That made Nat chuckle. "All right. I'll see to your injuries when you come out." Truthfully, he wanted to go into the shower with Ryu. But if he did, Ryu would probably insist on washing him again and it was Ryu who needed the attention. He decided to let him be for now and got his first aid things together while he waited for Ryu to finish.

When Ryu emerged from the bathroom, a towel swathed around his narrow hips, Nat caught his breath. The man's v-shaped torso, tattoos and all, made his mouth water each time he looked at him.

"Nat, do you mind if I put on the TV?"

"Of course not."

Ryu went over to the set and flicked it on. He went through the cable channels, stopping at a Japanese station. Nat couldn't understand the words but saw that the program was a newscast.

Ryu looked at him, a sheepish look in his eyes. "I don't care about the news really. I just wanted to hear Japanese."

Nat smiled at him and picked up a tube of first aid cream and some bandages. "No problem. Have a seat." He pointed to the bed where Ryu could sit and face the TV screen while Nat smeared some cream on the small cut above his eye. Ryu sat docile, letting him minister to him. He didn't even flinch or complain when Nat pressed on a sore spot and Nat noticed he seemed particularly quiet, as if he were in another world.

He recognised that kind of quiet, because he had always felt it too, after a fight. Time was needed to rest and come back, to make the transition from the intense concentration of boxing.

When he'd finished with the first aid cream, he picked up Ryu's bottle of oil, poured a few drops into one hand and began to massage Ryu's back and shoulders. Tension filled Ryu's wiry muscles and Nat squeezed gently, kneading Ryu's smooth skin in gentle yet firm circles until Ryu's body grew more pliant.

"Ohhh, that's really good, Nat."

"Enjoy."

Just touching Ryu made Nat's cock start to get hard. He really wanted to lay Ryu down and start licking various parts of his body, but Ryu didn't seem inclined towards sex at the moment...understandably, so Nat backed off a bit. "You're all set."

"Thanks, Nat." Ryu smiled at him then scooted back on the bed, reclining against the pillows. His attention seemed captured by the Japanese programming. The newscast had ended and some sort of ridiculous-looking game show had started. As with the newscast, Ryu didn't seem to care what the show was. Like he'd said, it wasn't the program that mattered, but the fact that it was from a familiar place.

Nat understood. He used to do a similar thing when he was younger and travelled to a foreign country to fight, like keeping a Thai newspaper with him or making sure he could get *pad thai* wherever he was.

Nat lowered himself to the floor and leaned back against the low bed. Quietly he watched the screen with Ryu, not caring that he didn't understand a word being said. Just sitting in Ryu's company was turning out to be a simple pleasure.

"Nat, can I ask you a question?"

Nat turned, leaning on the mattress. "Sure."

Ryu's gaze went to his for the first time since he'd begun to watch the TV. The Japanese game show droned on in the background, seemingly forgotten. "You almost got married once?"

"Yeah."

"Was she pretty?"

"She was pretty. And sweet."

Ryu nodded. "How long did you see each other?"

"About six months or so."

"How did you meet her?"

Nat felt like he was being interviewed for a magazine or something, but the sincerity in Ryu's face made him want to answer any question he asked.

"She was a professor at the university in Bangkok. We met because she was doing some sort of research on Thai society that included interviewing professional athletes and performers."

"Oh." Ryu looked thoughtful. "Did you like having...you know...sex...with her?"

Nat felt a tingle in his cheeks. Strange, he'd always felt awkward speaking about that subject. "Mostly I liked it. It felt good. But it wasn't...complete. I don't know how to explain it. Like something was missing."

Ryu nodded. "I understand." He looked straight at Nat. "I've never done it with a girl. I realised that wasn't going to happen when I was friends with O-Shin. The only time I wanted to kiss her was when she was dressed like a boy."

Nat chuckled. "Well, at least you were clear about it. No big identity conflicts, like Deena had. Deena!" Nat sat up straight. "I need to call her about tonight. Do you want to go?"

A shy look flashed through Ryu's eyes. "I guess."

Nat sat back, getting a tasty eyeful of Ryu's naked body stretched out on the bed, only his groin covered with the white towel. "Don't feel obligated."

"I never go to parties. I went to a few in high school, but that was it."

"Deena loves to throw parties. She always did, even when we were kids."

Ryu levered up on one elbow. "I'd go. Deena seems cool."

Nat smiled at him. "She is. Okay, I'll call and make sure it's just friends of hers coming." On impulse, he leaned over and pressed a kiss to Ryu's lips. When he pulled back, Ryu was staring at him. A chill went down his spine. "Should I not have done that?"

"You should have." Ryu looked down, seeming suddenly shy. To Nat's surprise, Ryu reached out and started toying with his hair. "I like your hair. It's soft."

Again, that flush of warmth in his chest that Ryu had given him from the moment they first met. "Thank you." Wishing his own introduction to Ryu's hair had been different, Nat opened his phone and dialled Deena's number. He turned around and leaned back, enjoying the soft tug of Ryu's fingers in his hair.

Deena answered on the third ring. "Nat, you're coming tonight, right?"

Nat laughed. "Hi, Deena. I'm fine thanks and how are you?"

"You know I don't bother with that crap. Are you coming?" She sounded really glad to hear from him in spite of her words. She'd always been that way, like pretending she hated Nat's and Aran's teasing when she was eating it up.

"We'll be there."

"Great! I'm looking forward to seeing that cutie pie of yours. You two look really good together, like you *fit*."

Nat's cheeks burned. He didn't say anything.

"Oh come on, Nat. Your silences speak louder than words. I saw how you were looking at him. Like you were floating in heaven." Pause. "Okay, I'll shut up. We'll discuss it later."

He looked straight ahead, vividly aware of Ryu's caress against his scalp. "See you tonight."

"Bye, Nat," Deena said in a mocking sing-song. In her own way she'd always been just as bad a tease. Only this time, she was serious. He knew her too well not to know that.

Heart speeding up, Nat shut the phone and sat back, eyes closed. Ryu's fingers remained stroking his hair and the contact sent pleasant shivers of warmth down his back.

Ryu remained quiet, seeming content just to touch his hair. "Thanks for answering my questions, Nat," he said after a few minutes.

"No problem." Nat thought briefly of Ruwee. There had been times since he broke off their relationship that he'd regretted it, thought that maybe he'd missed his chance at having something normal, something dependable.

But then, he realised, there was something more than normal and dependable in life that brought some sweetness to ease the suffering. Like the simple caress of someone's...Ryu's...fingers in his hair. Someone he wished he could just sit with like this, all the time. Someone like Ryu.

Unfortunately, life had never worked out how he wished.

So he'd just have to enjoy the few moments they had.

Chapter Ten

"Nat! There you are! Ooohhh and you brought the cutie pie!" Deena sashayed through the colourfully dressed crowd in her living room, wending her way between dancing couples and others standing around with drinks, chattering over the bass of the dance music.

She wore a shimmery dress that plunged down in front, showing cleavage, and her long hair swung loose around her shoulders. "I'm so glad to see both of you." She planted a kiss on Nat's cheek and smiled at Ryu.

Nat put an arm across Ryu's shoulders, aware that he might be uncomfortable. He was such a strange combination of things, Nat wasn't sure what to expect. He could be frightened and panicky one second, a fierce boxer in the next, then a passionate lover. "We can stay for a while."

Deena tugged both their hands. "You want something to drink? Thai iced tea?" She winked. "I know, without the spike in it." She pulled them both along through the crowd which was comprised mostly of the other *kathoeys* she was friends with and their companions. Nat glanced at Ryu. He was looking around as they moved through the small bungalow, but didn't look particularly uncomfortable. He breathed a small sigh of relief.

Ladling iced tea from a large punch bowl, she handed each of them a glass. "Take a few sips now, but then I want to dance with you guys."

Nat took a sip of the tea. "Where's Marco?"

"Not back from work yet, the poor guy. He'll be here."

"I like your house, Deena," Ryu said over the dance music.

Deena flashed a pleased smile at him. "Thanks, honey. I like it too. Marco and I are happy in our love nest. Now come on." She tugged Nat's hand, forcing him to set his drink down. He saw Ryu do the same and follow them out to the dance floor.

Immediately, Deena started swaying her hips and gyrating them, manoeuvring herself between Nat and Ryu.

Nat looked up at Ryu. To his surprise, Ryu had started moving his hips too in rhythmic circles. So! He could dance. Ryu was grinning back at him and raised his arms as he moved around to the music.

"Whoo!" Deena grasped Nat's hips and pulled him close while backing up towards Ryu. "This was just what I wanted. To be sandwiched in between you two!"

Ryu laughed. His eyes sparkled at Nat and he was obviously both enjoying himself and humouring his hostess. Nat let his own body sway with the rhythm. He'd never really been able to dance, but no one seemed to notice.

Deena stayed between them for several songs. Suddenly she waved her arms wildly in the direction of the front door. "Marco! You're here!" She turned to Nat. "'Scuse me, honey, I'm going to greet my man. You two enjoy. I'll introduce Ryu to him later." She danced off before Nat could answer.

Nat found himself facing Ryu. The music had slowed down. The bass was sinuous with a definitely erotic kind of beat. Ryu smiled at him, still winding his hips. He was wearing that black shirt over his hip-hugging jeans. Sweat glistened on his face and he was alluringly beautiful even with the small injuries marring his perfect complexion.

"You want to dance, Nat?"

Nat flicked a glance towards the other side of the room. Chuek stood there. He raised a glass of something he was drinking, probably soda water. He was doing his job, watching them while Tongmee covered the outside, watching the grounds. Strangely, he'd been more amicable after his sparring match with Ryu and hadn't had a problem with taking the outside watch at Deena's.

With everything in place, Nat looked back into Ryu's eyes and nodded. "Yeah, I'd like to dance." At first, he didn't reach out for Ryu, dancing close, without touching, but as the song wore on and the other people dancing around them pressed in closer, Nat dared to put his hands on Ryu's shoulders and draw their bodies together.

Mmm. Ryu was warm. His body heat simmered through his shirt and the scent of his woodsy oil filled the air, diffused by sweat. The bass of the music wound its way inside Nat. The soft lighting glowed off Ryu's skin and ebony hair and his lips were slightly parted. His hands now rested on Nat's hips and with each wind of his hips, his groin brushed across Nat's.

Heaven. Nat wondered if he was looking at Ryu now the way Deena had said he was doing in the restaurant. If so, then he was looking at Ryu the same way Ryu was looking up at him. Sort of with wonder, as if he couldn't believe what was happening and sort of…heavy-lidded, drunk with the moment.

More people must have come in while they were dancing because there was barely room to move. Deena sure knew a lot of people, but it was an advantage because Nat could press his chest to Ryu's as they danced without feeling too conspicuous. He could slide his hands from Ryu's shoulders around to his back and feel the wiry muscles shift with Ryu's graceful movements. There were so many people around them now, and someone had turned down the lights, because Nat could bend, unseen, into Ryu and brush his lips against the side of Ryu's neck, taste the salty-sweetness of his damp skin.

Hopefully no one saw Ryu tilt his head to the side, silently demanding more of Nat's petal-soft kisses on his neck. And hopefully, no one saw Ryu's hands slide from Nat's hips, over his chest and around to his back so that now their bodies were practically entwined on the dance floor.

Song after song passed. No one tried to come up and make introductions, as if the people around them were leaving him and Ryu alone in their little space, in this sudden cocoon that seemed to be around them. Just once, Nat glanced up and saw Deena close by, similarly entwined with Marco. She winked at him and kept dancing.

* * * *

Tongmee's cell phone rang. He glanced back at the house, full of people and music, and then opened his phone. No one would hear him out on the walkway. It was Suzuki.

"Tongmee."

"I'm in Phuket. I'll be in the Royal Hotel, room 315 by, say, one a.m."

Tongmee checked his watch. It was almost midnight. Nat had been in there for quite a while. "I'm not sure what time I'll be able to deliver him. They're at some party and I can't secure him until we leave and get back to the place they're staying. I'll let you know as soon as I'm on the way with him."

"I'll be there."

Tongmee snapped his phone shut. Just as quickly, it rang again. This time it was Phoenix. "Tongmee."

"Hey, we're getting ready to leave. About five minutes."

"No problem. I'm right outside on the front walk."

"Thank you. And would you please call Seinalloy and Pettoh and tell them we'll be back soon?"

"Sure, Agent Phoenix." He hung up the phone and put it back in his pocket. There was no need to call those two. They wouldn't answer anyway. Too much tranquilizer in the food he'd brought them before leaving for this party. Seinalloy and Pettoh would be out for at least another couple of hours. At least.

* * * *

"Time to go," Nat murmured in Ryu's ear. They'd actually had a great time. Ryu seemed happy. He'd gotten along really well with Deena and Marco and was turning out to be quite charming in a social setting, Nat noticed with a pang. Ryu worked in a hotel that serviced men sexually. He made a living at being charming.

Not going there, he thought as he led Ryu towards their hostess to say goodnight. He just wanted to get Ryu back to their room and make love to him. All this close dancing and hip grinding had him hard enough to cut diamonds and all he wanted was to feel Ryu, taste him and bury his cock deep inside him.

Deena walked them to the front door. "I'm so glad you guys came. I'm sorry you have to leave. Come to the restaurant tomorrow, okay?"

Nat put a hand on her shoulder. "If we can. In any case, thanks so much for a fun time."

Deena winked. "That's what I'm here for. A good time." She kissed Nat's cheek and then kissed Ryu's. "Thanks for coming, Ryu. It's really good to know you."

Ryu smiled. "Thank you. You too."

"Get home safe."

Nat smiled at her. "We will." Good thing that the other agents would be in the car with them, because otherwise, they wouldn't get home at all.

* * * *

As soon as the door to their room closed, Ryu felt his back being pressed against it and Nat's lips closing over his, hot and wanting. Nat's hands slid from his shoulders and started working open the buttons on his shirt. Ryu could feel the tremble in Nat's hands as he answered the heated slide of the larger man's tongue with his.

Kiku never wanted me like this. The words passed through Ryu's fevered mind as he sagged against the door. Kiku had resisted him at first. And yes, he'd obviously enjoyed the sex, but he could have taken or left it. At least that's how it had seemed.

It sure as hell didn't feel that way with Nat. The way Nat looked at him, touched him, responded to him in all ways — hungrily, yet passionately sweet, like he'd been waiting for him all his life.

Nat got all the buttons undone and slid his hands over Ryu's chest, soft circles that rubbed his nipples into hardness. Ryu moaned into Nat's mouth. The sound only seemed to urge Nat on, sending his hands down Ryu's stomach to his belt buckle.

Weakness saturated Ryu. He gave himself up to this delicious ravaging, savouring the feeling of being so *wanted*. Nat's tongue swirled hungrily against his, suckling and nipping like a beast in heat. He didn't even care that Nat was just releasing his pent up longing, the desire he'd kept hidden for most of his life. There was a sweetness in it, like Nat felt safe enough with him to let it out.

Nat had gotten his jeans undone and hooked his fingertips under the strings of Ryu's underwear, sliding it down past his knees. Nat's hands slid over Ryu's hips, then squeezed his ass. A deep groan vibrated in Ryu's mouth, a sound that conveyed Nat's appreciation of what he was touching and squeezing.

He reached for Nat's jeans, intending to undo them and drop to his knees. But Nat grasped his wrists and broke their kiss. In the light filtering through the window, Nat's eyes were glazed and his ragged breathing was louder than the air conditioner. "Let *me*, Ryu. Please."

Ryu stared at him. A tendril of discomfort snaked through his middle. This wasn't the usual. Habit had taken over, the habit of pleasuring, but Nat was stopping him. The pleading sound of his words made him yield, made him let Nat lower his hands to his sides.

Nat kissed him again and Ryu could feel the swollenness of both their lips as they chafed together. Nat's scent, male and musky filled his nostrils, gave him that slightly drunken feeling it always did. He sagged back against the door again, and let Nat do whatever it was he'd had in mind. His heart raced and his dragon was so tight it could spear through wood, holding him captive in the grip of need.

Nat pulled away from their kiss again and knelt swiftly down.

Ryu pulled in a breath. He reached out, an impulse to stop him, but when his fingertips landed on Nat's hair, Nat only dove forward and captured the head of his cock in his mouth. Ohhh, like a moist hot glove that sucked him into sweet oblivion! Ryu's eyelids shuttered and he sagged harder against the door, anchored in place only by Nat's large hands on his ass cheeks.

Nat plunged down and swallowed his whole dragon, right to his pubic hair. The movement was hungry, greedy, like Ryu's cock was the best thing he'd ever tasted. Nat's lips tightened, making him groan and pant. *Kuso!* He felt his eyes roll back in his head, which now lolled over to one side. "Nat," he whispered. That's all he could say as ecstasy engulfed him.

Nat's hands squeezed his ass, kneaded the muscles in a way that showed he was appreciating that part of him too. Then he slid back and swallowed Ryu's cock again to the base. Ryu pulled in a breath and felt the soft vibration of a moan around the stalk of his dragon. His eyes rolled back again and he clasped Nat's head, felt the sleekness of his hair, let his fingertips explore the muscles in Nat's jaw working as he sucked his cock.

One of Nat's hands crept further back and his fingers dipped into the crevice. Ryu pulled in a breath as Nat's fingertips found his hole and caressed it. One fingertip pushed its way in, not deep, but enough to send sparks through his balls.

Ryu moaned again. If Nat kept that up, he'd come within a minute. When Nat had touched him there before, it had driven him so wild with pleasure he hadn't felt in too long. Now it felt incredible again.

Nat pushed his finger in deeper and tightened his lips at the same time. He was sucking harder and faster, sliding to the head and back to the base of Ryu's cock in a fevered rhythm now. Through half-closed lids, Ryu watched Nat's head moving in the shadowy light. The pressure was building, more with each tiny push of Nat's finger and suck of his mouth.

He meant to pull back, meant not to let his climax gush into Nat's mouth, but Nat held him firmly in place and drank him down. Ryu could feel the muscles of Nat's throat work as he swallowed, his hands caressing Ryu's ass until he'd drank down every last drop and then pulled away, panting.

Nat rested his hands on Ryu's ass. The tang of Ryu's cum rolled on his tongue and Ryu's woodsy oil scent was on his skin, diffused into the air along with the smell of sex. It made his cock throb painfully. He'd always enjoyed sex, but the way he'd devoured Ryu's cock, swallowed every bit of cum that splashed out of him like it was a magic potion...

Ryu's fingers trembled against his scalp, caressed his hair as if he'd been shaken by the way Nat had gone down on him. "Nat."

The shaky whisper made him look up. "Are you all right?"

To his relief, Ryu's sensual lips turned up in a smile. "I'm more than all right. I want you to fuck me."

The words shivered through Nat's whole body, right to the tip of his achingly hard cock.

Before he could answer Ryu had shifted to the side, struggling with his boots and his jeans that were bunched around his calves. "Come on," he whispered harshly. "Get undressed."

Wordlessly, Nat obeyed. He stripped off his shirt, then yanked off his sandals and jeans. His cock sprung gratefully out of the confining denim and he'd barely turned around when Ryu was standing there with his bottle of oil. Damn, he'd moved really fast.

Just as quickly, Ryu slathered the oil up and down the length of Nat's cock. The slide of his hand all slick with oil made Nat groan and he had to restrain himself from yanking Ryu to the floor and turning him over.

He didn't need to. In the next second, Ryu reached back and put the oil on his ass then went to his knees, kneeling over the side of the bed. "Please hurry, Nat."

In a hot second, he was down behind him, covering Ryu's back with his chest. Just the heat of their bare skin and muscles together was a high, never mind the heat that engulfed his cock as it slid between Ryu's ass cheeks.

Ryu's knees were far apart, rendering him stretched and open. He panted as soon as Nat dappled his fingertips over his hole and pushed the head of his cock against the puckered skin. "Nat, yesss." Ryu's voice was a hiss and made him wild, as if he could slide right in hard and that would be perfect.

Ryu pushed back against him, a demanding push that whipped his thoughts away. He grabbed Ryu's hips and thrust. Hard. Their bodies slammed together. Ryu cried out and pumped against him, not waiting a second for Nat to find a rhythm. Ryu squeezed his ass muscles and kept thrusting against him, as if he were trying to get Nat off without Nat having to move.

Each squeeze sent darts of heat through Nat's entire lower body, ass, balls, cock, thighs. He grasped Ryu's hips tighter, his fear of hurting Ryu gone. Ryu's hands gripped the bedding and he seemed to be anchoring himself so he could push back even harder.

That alone sent Nat closer to the edge. Sweat dripped down his face, into his eyes. He felt the salty moisture cover his body, make him slide against Ryu's sleekly muscled body. He didn't care about anything else except Ryu underneath him, surrounding his cock with tight friction. His mind was blank, not even full of twinkling lights. There was no world left around them. Only him and Ryu...

He groaned as the pressure exploded. With his cheek pressed to Ryu's back, his eyes shut, he kept thrusting. One spasm after the next ploughed through his cock, made his mind spiral away. Ryu was pushing against him, squeezing him, milking every drop from him. Nothing had ever felt so incredible in his life, almost like they were one body.

And then it was over. He sagged down on top of Ryu, squeezing him close, breathing in his scent. Damn, if this moment could just last forever —

Bam! Sudden blinding pain shot through his head. *Bam!* Blunt pressure connected with his skull. He released Ryu and slid off him, feeling his body hit the cold floor.

Then the world went black.

Chapter Eleven

"Nat!" Ryu whipped around.

Nat was lying in a heap, not moving.

"Nat!" He leaned over and saw a dark trickle down Nat's temple. He was hurt, bad. "I'll get help."

A clicking sound by his head made him freeze. Something hard pushed against his skull. A gun. "You're not getting help. You're getting dressed. Now."

Holy shit. Ryu looked up. In the shadowy light a dark figure stood above him. The man's breathing was tight and a crazy energy radiated off of him.

Tongmee.

Before Ryu could move, the man's other hand swung around and something pricked him in the back. Hard.

"Ah!" He'd had enough shots in his life to recognise the jab of a needle.

"Get dressed you little bitch." Tongmee poked his head with the gun.

His heart raced, clawed towards his throat, but he couldn't let Nat die. "No. I need to help Nat."

"He'll be fine, as long as you stay away from him, you diseased little fuck. Get dressed or I'll shoot him. Somewhere it'll hurt him bad." Tongmee pointed the gun towards Nat's unconscious form.

Without thinking, Ryu shot to his feet. Hot tears stung at his eyes but he groped through the pile of clothes he and Nat had left on the floor and picked out his black shirt first.

His eyes didn't leave the gun trained towards Nat as he struggled to button up his shirt. Whatever Tongmee had injected him with was making his brain woozy. His hands felt like they were made of cotton.

"Hurry up."

"What are you doing?" he heard himself ask as he grasped for his underwear. To think, this guy had snuck in and stood over them while they had sex, waiting to clobber Nat.

"Just hurry up."

Ryu stumbled. His body was growing heavier. He slipped on his underwear and then fumbled with his jeans. In the background, he heard more clicking sounds and saw Tongmee bent over Nat, handcuffing Nat's wrists to the iron bed. He wanted to lunge at Tongmee, grab the gun from his hand but he could barely move. His eyes grew heavier and he fell on his hands and knees. He reached for one boot, but couldn't…quite…reach…

* * * *

Ryu was in trouble.

Kiku sat bolt upright, making the water of the bath slosh around. His heart pounded and a cold sweat broke out on his skin in spite of the steamy heat of the room.

"Kiku, what is it?" Yuzo's hands had slipped away from his massage of Kiku's shoulders and now his huge eyes were wide.

"I don't know. I just know that Ryu's in trouble." He vaulted from the tub and grabbed his towel, throwing it around his hips. "I'm going down there immediately." Without bothering with his slippers, he charged from the room.

"Kiku, I'll go with you." Yuzo was already behind him.

He swung around and grasped Yuzo's arms. "No. You need to stay here and watch the phone. In case Ryu tries to reach me. I'll tell the agents. I'll need one of them to drive me to the airport. I'll be ready in a few minutes. There's no time to make other arrangements."

Yuzo nodded, wide-eyed. "Okay."

Back in his room, Kiku threw on a pair of jeans and a T-shirt. "Please, let him be all right," he muttered as he stuffed a few things into a carry-on bag. He'd never forgive himself if anything happened to Ryu. He also didn't know how he'd go on. As much as he loved Yuzo, Ryu was deeply a part of him, their lives almost one life, they were so close. Ryu's presence made life bearable, gave it joy in the midst of madness. Ryu was and had been so many things to him. A little brother, a lover, a friend, a son...

"There's a car waiting to take you right now. The agents cleared a flight for you."

Kiku whipped around. Yuzo stood in the doorway, looking frightened. Yuzo, too, had come to like Ryu very much. All the White Tigers there loved him. "Thanks, Yuzo."

Yuzo nodded and stepped aside so he could pass. Kiku stopped long enough to press a quick kiss to his lips then rushed down the stairs. He probably wasn't going to get there in time to prevent something from happening to Ryu, but at least Agent Phoenix was there.

His silent prayers continued as he slid into the car and closed the door. Then all the way to the airport and grabbing a flight to Bangkok. It would have cost a shitload to take a flight on such short notice, but now he didn't need the wad of cash with him that Ryu's father had had delivered to the White Tiger that afternoon. Along with a note that promised protection and expressed great sorrow.

That would lift Ryu's spirits, knowing his father had responded. As long as nothing bad happened to his little sweet friend.

Life would become very dark if something bad happened to Ryu. Very dark.

* * * *

Ryu opened his eyes. The world was blurry and his body felt heavy, drugged,

like someone had poured lead through his arms and legs.

"Finally, you're awake."

That voice. That familiar horrible, snake voice.

Ryu pulled in a breath. Prickles of energy pulled him from this drugged state, infused him with consciousness.

Suzuki.

How the hell? He blinked again and felt the scratchiness of material under his bare skin.

Bare?

He shot upright. The air in the room swirled around his body. He looked down. And froze. He was almost naked. Someone had stripped him down to his g-string and left him on this bed.

A chuckle. Suzuki again.

Ryu turned and his heart nearly clawed its way to his throat. Suzuki sat in a chair nearby, next to a small table.

A hotel room. They were in a hotel room. Oh shit. Where was Nat?

Then he remembered. His last memory before Tongmee had jabbed him with a needle full of some kind of tranquilizer. Nat, handcuffed to the bed, unconscious, and the trail of blood down one temple where Tongmee struck him with the butt of his gun.

Now, Ryu was alone. Horribly, wretchedly alone with a rapist. *His* rapist. And no doubt there were goons on the other side of this door. With guns. He swallowed though his throat and mouth were so dry he almost choked.

"I don't understand why you're so afraid of me, Ryu." Suzuki rose from the chair. He looked the same as always. Stocky, like a bulldog, and crazy. "Why be afraid of someone who thinks you're so fine? Who really appreciates you? Kiku never appreciated you. He likes having you around to wash dishes and wipe his ass. But he really prefers Yuzo. Right?"

The words stung like darts, but Ryu only stared at him. Suzuki already had an erection tenting the front of his trousers and his thick hands were working open the buttons of his shirt as he came towards the bed.

Suzuki dropped his shirt on the foot of the bed and pulled off his socks, leaving them on the floor. "You think I was trying to hurt you that night. But I meant it to feel good. Then you would have known I'm right for you, Ryu. You were just too young to understand."

Ryu stared at him, fighting to keep his breath normal. Icy sweat erupted in his armpits. How the hell was he going to keep Suzuki from raping him again? If he fought back, the guy's goons would come in and hold him down with a gun to his head. Even if he got away from them, they'd shoot him.

Suzuki lifted off his undershirt. "If you just give me a chance, Ryu, you'd see that I'm good for you." Greedy hunger glittered in his small eyes. The scary part was, Ryu sensed that Suzuki believed what he was saying. Somewhere in the man's twisted mind and heart, he believed he cared.

Suzuki's hands went to his belt. He pulled it open and undid his pants. Ryu's eye fell on the cell phone clipped to one pocket as the pants dropped to the floor and Suzuki stepped out of them. "I tell you what, Ryu." Clad in only his white underwear, erection bulging through, and body tattoos that stretched to his wrists and ankles, Suzuki sat next to him on the bed and stroked one thigh.

His touch made Ryu feel like bugs crawled on his skin but he didn't move, didn't let his revulsion show. "What are you going to tell me?" he managed to say.

"Well, I know you don't realise you could like me. But you will. In the meantime, I'll sweeten things for you. You stay with me and I'll leave Kiku alone. I won't even take another yen from him." He slid his fingertips to the top of Ryu's thigh, acting like he was going to touch his dragon.

Ryu squelched the impulse to scoot back. His life was at stake and there was no room for error. "You mean that, Taro-san? You'd let him go?" Of course, he didn't believe Suzuki for a second, but whatever it took…

Suzuki's eyes lit up. "Absolutely. That's all I ever really wanted, you know." He squeezed Ryu's thigh and then brushed a thumb over the head of his cock where it pushed out the cloth pouch of the g-string.

Ryu felt a surge of tears. He fought them back. *Have…to…stay…calm.* "It is?"

"Don't be stupid." Suzuki's thumb pressed down on his cock. "Of course."

Ouch. Ryu blinked hard to push back the discomfort. Suzuki was a sadist and Ryu tried not to think of the possible reasons Yuzo had run from him in terror.

"Kiku has filled your head with shit. You think he's some kind of god but he's a stupid prick. A lowlife opportunist. You don't know him as I do."

The words stung even though they weren't true. But they didn't hurt as much as Suzuki's thumb and forefinger squeezing his cock.

Ryu forced himself to smile and nod. "I'll take that trade, Taro-san. I'd be happy to."

Suzuki cocked his head to one side. "Such a sudden change of heart. Is it that you like this?" He pinched down.

Ryu cried out. The pain made him breathless. He needed to answer. Needed to pretend. "Yes. You...were right. Wow."

Suzuki turned and climbed fully onto the bed, facing him. Before Ryu could think, Suzuki grasped both his arms and yanked him forward, forcing him to straddle Suzuki's lap. Suzuki's eyelids shuttered. "Ahhh, finally." He pulled Ryu close, making their cocks rub together. His large hands pulled on Ryu's back, forced him firmly in place. "Hold me, Ryu."

With his heart pounding so hard he felt like he'd black out, Ryu obeyed. He slipped his hands around the other man's thick body.

Suzuki's hot breath fanned over his chest. He felt the moist lick of the other man's tongue as he found one nipple. Ryu pulled in a breath. The feeling of Suzuki in his arms was hideous. Monstrous.

Suzuki bit down on his nipple.

Ryu sucked in a breath. He could barely hold back the tears as pain, fear and horror engulfed him. Without thinking, he began to rub his hands in circles on Suzuki's back.

Suzuki murmured against Ryu's chest. "Mmm, that feels so good. My beautiful Ryu."

Ryu trembled as he rubbed. Harder, more firmly. Suzuki was moaning, and his body relaxed in Ryu's arms.

That's when he realised it. What to do. His breath nearly stopped. How could he? His conscience gave a sharp pang. Even to Suzuki, how could he?

Then he remembered. *The pain, the humiliation. Taro's strong grip, the agonizing shove of his cock in the most sensitive part of him. The other hand clamped over his mouth.* Anger surged, tingled down his arms into his hands as they kneaded Suzuki's fleshy back. More memories came. *Kiku's mangled hand, the way he'd bled and suffered. The fear they all lived with everyday because of this man...*Who knew if he'd even survive the night with Suzuki?

Ryu's breath rose and fell heavily as he positioned his fingertips, just the way Kiku had shown him all those years ago. *Push down hard*, Kiku had said. *And don't let up until it's done.*

Suzuki groaned. Ryu jumped, heart pounding mercilessly, before he realised it was a groan of pleasure. Breathing heavily, he repositioned his hands.

He squeezed his eyes shut. Pulled in a deep breath.

And pushed. Hard.

Suzuki groaned again. His body stiffened, his hands tightened on Ryu's back, as if realising what was happening to him.

Ryu pushed harder.

A small choking gurgle issued from Suzuki's throat and then he went limp.

Ryu gasped. Prickles of fear crawled through every nerve ending in his body. He barely breathed, trying to register any sign of life in the other man's body. Had he done it? He dared to release the pressure. Suzuki remained the way he was, sagging heavily against Ryu, so hard it pushed him back against the headboard. Ryu put his fingertips to the man's neck, feeling for a pulse. Nothing.

Suzuki was...

Oh shit. Terror made his body feel like a block of ice. His glance flickered to the door of the bedroom. Suzuki always kept two armed goons with him wherever he went and no doubt, they were there now, on the other side of that door. They'd shoot him in a heartbeat when they knew their boss was dead. He looked around for his clothes. They were gone, as were his shoes. One glance out the window showed him he was too high up to jump out. He was trapped.

The phone.

Suzuki's cell phone was on the floor with his pants. Ryu pushed and Suzuki's body fell away, collapsed on the mattress. Snatching the phone from the belt, Ryu dialled Kiku's number. He didn't know Nat's number by heart.

His heart pounded and tears slipped down his cheeks as the phone rang and rang. No answer. But Kiku's voice mail picked up. "Kiku," he whispered when it beeped, "I'm here with Suzuki. In a hotel room. He looked at a card on the nightstand table. "The Royal Hotel, room 310. Someone locked Nat in our room at the training camp. Suwat Training Camp. He's hurt. I don't even know if he's alive. I don't know the address. Please, where are you? Suzuki is...I did that nerve press you showed me. Please help me." He snapped the phone shut then opened it again and called home.

Someone picked up on the second ring. "*Moshi moshi*, White Tiger," a familiar voice answered.

Ryu's heart lurched. "Yuzo."

"Ryu? Is that you?"

Yuzo's voice practically made him cry from relief. "Yuzo, where's Kiku? I tried calling him but he didn't answer."

"He's on a plane to Thailand. He said you're in trouble."

"I am." In whispers, he explained what had happened.

"Don't worry, Ryu, Kiku already has people on the way. I'll tell the agent here where you are. Someone will come rescue you soon. Listen, Taro always has a gun in his jacket. Take his gun out and keep it with you. Okay?" Yuzo sounded terribly frightened.

"Yes, thank you."

In the background he heard Yuzo telling the agent where he was. "Ryu, they know now where you are. Someone will be there as soon as possible. Do you want me to stay on the phone with you? Will it help?"

"I'm afraid they'll hear me if I do."

"Okay. Call back if you need me. Okay? Now get the gun."

"Thank you, Yuzo."

He hung up and tiptoed to the chair where Suzuki's jacket was. Just as Yuzo had said, the small gun was there. Kiku had once shown him how to fire a gun. He returned to the bed, the gun in one hand, the phone clutched in the other. Quietly, he slipped back onto the bed then lay down, positioning himself with Suzuki's body spooning his so that it would look like they were asleep together. *Please, Kiku. Please. Help me.* He prayed over and over. The silent prayer was the only thing that brought him any comfort. Any hope.

And then he closed his eyes. And waited.

Chapter Twelve

"Agent Phoenix! Are you in there?"

Nat blinked as the voice penetrated the blackness. He raised his head.

"Agent Phoenix!"

Nat recognised Seinalloy's voice as the agent pounded on the door. The sound reverberated through Nat's skull with blinding pain. "Yeah, I'm here," he managed to call. He yanked against the handcuffs, but they held him fast to headboard. "Get a key from Lew and get in here with a pair of bolt cutters!"

"Yes, sir."

Blood had dried on his temple and cheek. Nat could feel it as he crouched and waited for Seinalloy to come back with a key to the room.

"Hold on, Agent Phoenix." The key fumbled in the lock and then the door opened. "Phoenix, holy shit!" Seinalloy charged in and knelt down. "Are you all right? Do you need medical attention?"

"No. How about you?"

"I'm okay. The others are too. But Tongmee...he must have drugged our food and took our cell phones. He has one of the cars and disabled the other one. We all just woke up. I've already called headquarters from Lew's office. Pettoh and Chuek went to the police to get backup."

"Where's Ryu?"

"Tongmee must have taken him. He's gone. But we know where Ryu is. He's alive, Nat, as far as we know."

Fuck! His head pounded with an excruciating ache, but the pain was nothing compared to what Tongmee would be feeling when Nat got his hands on the bastard.

"Who told you where he is?" Nat's heart raced like mad as Seinalloy snipped the handcuffs with the bolt cutter and then cut each wrist cuffs.

"When we alerted headquarters they told us they received a call from the White Tiger place in Tokyo. Someone there had heard from Ryu, telling them where he was."

Ryu. Nat's body was in a cold sweat of fear for him. The bonds dropped away and Nat fell forward. Every muscle in his body protested. "Where is he?" Nat refused an offer of assistance to get up. He managed to unfold his body from the floor and grab at his clothes, which still lay in a pile nearby. At least Tongmee hadn't taken them.

"The Royal Hotel, room 315."

"Good work. We have to get the hell out of here. Tongmee could kill him. He's crazed." *If he hasn't already.*

The stiffness worked out of his muscles as he dressed, enough to give him energy to charge out the door and almost collide with Lew. Icy fear rippled over every inch of Nat's body. God only knew what Tongmee had done with Ryu. Shit, he'd needed to be more careful. He should have replaced Tongmee immediately upon seeing the man's mental state.

"Nat, are you all right?" Lew steadied them both with hands on Nat's arms.

"I'm fine. Have to go, Lew." He released Lew and sprinted to the driveway.

Out front, a police car had pulled up and he and Seinalloy piled in. "There's no time to get more agents from Bangkok. Tell your other cars to meet us at the Royal Hotel. No sirens. They'll hear us coming and clear out. Station officers at every exit and in the lobby. Wait until I get there for further orders."

Within ten minutes, they were at the curb of the hotel.

Nat leaped out and signalled to Seinalloy to make sure their backup was in place. "Seinalloy, I want Pettoh and Chuek to back me up. We're going to the suite. I'll pose as room service and then we bust in."

"Yes, sir."

After putting on bulletproof vests, Nat took Seinalloy and three police officers up the elevator to the third floor. In front of the door he'd been told was the suite where Suzuki held Ryu, he signalled to them all then unholstered his gun, clicking off the safety. His heart hammering in his chest, he took a deep breath and knocked on the door.

"*Nande?*" a man said in Japanese from the other side, probably asking who it was.

"Room service," Nat said in English.

After a few seconds, he heard the lock slid open and the door cracked. A man's face appeared in the space. "Room service?" he repeated.

"Special from manager."

The door opened a bit more then the man's eyes went wide and he tried to slam it shut.

But Nat kicked it open, gun brandished and charged in. "Police!"

The man who'd opened the door reached for a gun in his holster but Nat tackled him. With a grunt, the guy landed on the floor, Nat on top of him. "Freeze!" Nat yelled and put his gun to the guy's head. Behind him, Seinalloy and the officers charged in. A shot was fired. Nat heard the bullet zing past his head and go into the doorpost. But in the next second, Seinalloy had the shooter on his stomach on the floor and was on top of him, surrounded by the backup officers.

"Take this guy," Nat said to two officers. Immediately, they were there, both guns pointed to his head and one knelt down to cuff him so Nat could get up.

Brandishing his gun again, he approached the closed door that led to the next room of the suite. He reached out and tried the knob. Locked. Without a word, he kicked the door in, gun pointed.

Suzuki was there on the bed. Behind him, Nat saw a flash of another thigh, inked with tattoos. He recognised the colours and patterns immediately. Ryu. *Lord Buddha let him be alive.*

"Suzuki, freeze!" he yelled in English.

Suzuki didn't respond.

With his gun pointed at Suzuki's head, Nat moved closer. "Get off the bed with your hands up or I'll shoot."

Still, no movement.

Nat leaned over and tapped Suzuki's foot. Nothing. His gaze moved up the man's heavy tattooed body. Chest and back were unmoving.

Suzuki was dead.

Dead?

Dear lord, Ryu.

Nat lowered the gun and inched around the side of the bed. He could hear breathing. Short, soft, panicky sounding breaths. Ryu was stretched out next to Suzuki, wearing only his g-string. Suzuki's body cradled his as if they'd been sleeping.

Ryu's eyes were open.
Nat exhaled the sharp sweetness of relief and knelt down.
Ryu was staring at him. "Nat," he whispered.
"I'm here, Ryu. You're safe now."
Ryu blinked as if he didn't understand the word 'safe.' Then his eyes closed and he went limp.

* * * *

Ryu's eyes popped open. Kiku's face hovered above him. *I died*, he thought. *I'm dead.* How else could he be seeing Kiku when Kiku was in Tokyo?

Kiku's dark eyes misted over. Lines of obvious worry creased his forehead. "Ryu, thank God. He reached out and Ryu felt the warm brush of Kiku's hand on his cheek.

Ryu went to speak but his mouth was so dry his tongue stuck to the roof of his mouth. In the next second, Kiku lifted a glass of water and held it to his lips. Kiku was sitting next to him. *Alive.* Was he still lying in the bed where he'd been with Suzuki?

He accepted a sip of water and heaved a deep breath, feeling the softness of a mattress under his back. The material brushed his skin. Oh, he was still almost naked, but covered by a sheet and blanket…and still unconvinced this wasn't a weird dream. "How did you find me?"

"When I arrived in Phuket, I got your voice mail. I went to that hotel but you'd already been brought here. Agent Phoenix's people told me where you were and gave me the address. A taxi brought me the rest of the way."

177

Ryu blinked. Kiku's weight was sinking the mattress. His familiar scent was in the air around them. He was really here. Which meant that they were both alive. Strange, he didn't feel so relieved to be alive. A dark feeling had settled inside him, not letting him feel free. His hands felt the ghostly pressure of Suzuki's nerve endings as he'd pressed the life out of the man. "Where am I?" he whispered.

Kiku set the glass down. His face reflected worry and Ryu knew that Kiku sensed his inner darkness. "You're in the house of someone named Deena."

Deena. Nat's friend. "Where's Nat?"

"He's here." Kiku indicated the doorway. He turned. "Agent Phoenix," he said in English, "Ryu's asking for you."

Apparently Nat spoke English too. So did he. Kiku made sure they were all proficient in the language because so many guests came from the United States and from the UK.

Nat hovered in the doorway, a strange look on his face, as if he were hesitant to come in. But when their gazes locked he came over to the bed, standing behind Kiku, a worried look in his large eyes. "How do you feel, Ryu?"

Ryu blinked back a sudden rush of tears. "Like shit. I'm a murderer now."

Kiku's hand grasped his and squeezed it.

Nat moved in closer, and dropped to his knees by the bed. "You're not a murderer, Ryu. What you did was in self-defence."

The tears came then, as if Nat's assurance had given him permission not to feel like the biggest scum in the world. Just like the scum he had spent his life working so hard not to be. "He was hurting me."

Kiku's hand tightened on his and through Ryu's tears, he saw his friend's deep anger and distress. He knew Kiku blamed himself.

"You were very brave, Ryu," Nat said. "You kept your head in a terrifying situation. Better than most could do. I swear."

"That's the truth," Kiku said. "Everything Agent Phoenix is saying is the absolute truth."

Ryu saw Nat glance up at Kiku.

"Look at the two of you, hovering over the poor guy."

Ryu looked up with Nat and Kiku. Deena stood in the doorway, holding a tray with a bowl of something hot steaming on it.

"Move back," she said, coming in. "Give little Ryu some air." She smiled at him as Kiku released his hand and obediently moved away. As did Nat.

"Here's some *tom ka*." Deena perched on the bed where Kiku had been, bowl in hand and fed him a spoonful. Warm spicy coconut milk flooded his tongue. Very good. She smiled. "There you go, honey. Deena will fix you right up."

Ryu heard Nat chuckle and couldn't help smiling as a second spoonful of milky soup headed towards his mouth. He felt like a prince being the centre of three people's attention at once. And it had been a lot more than that earlier. Cops and agents and criminals. All centred around him.

Kiku and Nat were both standing nearby, watching Deena feed him the soup. The two men of his dreams, right here, hovering over him, looking worried.

"I can hold the bowl, Deena, it's okay."

"You just rest. I'll take care of it."

"You're in good hands, Ryu," Nat said. "I have to…go away for a bit."

Ryu looked at him. A sudden ache nagged at him in a way he couldn't put words to. "Where are you going?"

Nat sighed. "I have to find Tongmee. He's out there somewhere. I need to deal with him." He looked down.

"Don't blame yourself, Agent Phoenix. You needed to be able to trust someone in your command."

Nat's head shot up, eyes wide. It was obvious he was surprised at Kiku's mind-reading ability.

"Nat." Ryu tried to sit up but his body wouldn't let him. Exhaustion wrung every ounce of strength he had. "Let Kiku help you. He'll be able to find him." He looked at his old friend. "Can't you?"

"I don't know. I'd need to have something he touched."

Wilting back against the bed, he returned Kiku's gaze. "He touched *me*." Grabbed, dragged, drugged, was more like it.

Kiku nodded. "I don't know if Agent Phoenix understands."

Nat looked between Ryu and Fujimara. He'd been completely unprepared for the impact of meeting the man Ryu was in love with. Fujimara had arrived at Deena's shortly after Nat had settled Ryu into this bed and was sitting at the bedside, holding Ryu's hand. When Fujimara had walked in, Nat had Set Ryu's hand down on the mattress, as if caught with another man's lover and gotten up, making space for him to see Ryu. He'd remained hovering in the doorway, wanting to come back in and feeling as if he just couldn't.

Now, he ached with a dark feeling, as if Ryu was slipping away from him, just when…"I don't understand, Ryu, but if you have a way to find him, I'll listen. Tongmee is dangerous."

He almost killed someone very important to me. The words hovered on Nat's lips but he couldn't say them. Maybe it was Fujimara's presence that stopped him. Even though physically, he was the same size as Nat, his spirit seemed to fill the room with a kind of simmering energy. "What do you need to do?" he asked in English.

"I need to touch Ryu and see what's there. This man will have left an impression in him from the contact."

"Okay. Deena, let him in."

"All right." Deena set down the bowl on the nightstand and moved away. "But after this, let him rest, all right?"

"I promise."

He watched Fujimara sit back down on the bed and pick up Ryu's hand. For several moments, Fujimara said nothing, eyes closed as he held Ryu's hand between both of his. "He's a thin guy, angry-looking, correct?" Fujimara asked in English.

Nat's heart jumped. "Yes."

"I see him. He's kneeling in front of an altar. There's a...photograph on the altar with a picture."

Nat caught his breath. Prickles of heat travelled down his back. "Do you see anything else? Who's in the photo?"

"It looks like a man. A young man. And there are flowers around the picture as well as a...well, it looks like an urn."

Nat froze. Tongmee's brother. Nat had seen the altar in Tongmee's mother's house. He lived in a suburb of Bangkok. *Tongmee was at home.* He really was crazy. As if he was waiting for someone to come and catch him. "I have to go now." He squelched the overwhelming desire to fall to his knees at the bedside and kiss Ryu's lips. Something told him he'd better get used to doing without that. Those kisses...and more...had been a sweet couple of days, but now, Fujimara was here and Ryu would no doubt remember how much in love he was with the guy.

Although...Ryu did look upset. "Are you coming back?"

"I'll come back here. I promise."

With a last look into those sweet eyes, Nat turned around and rushed out. He could only pray that Tongmee stayed where he was.

* * * *

"Are you sure Nat's going to be okay?" Ryu closed his eyes. He rested his head against Kiku's thigh. He felt so like a little kid and didn't want to, but he couldn't help it. Terror still coursed through him. Terror, guilt, disgust. And fear for Nat. Tongmee *was* a murderer. In his heart.

Kiku's steady caress on his hair was the only thing that made him feel okay in that moment.

"For the thousandth time, Ryu, Nat will be fine. I beg you to believe that."

Ryu yawned. He'd fought sleep for the last several hours, knowing that Nat was going into another dangerous situation. Now, he was beginning to lose the battle. He was still disappointed that Nat hadn't kissed him good-bye. But why should he have kissed him? Just because they'd had incredible sex for a couple of days under intense circumstances, didn't mean Nat was in love with him. Or he with Nat...

He couldn't think straight. Couldn't get past the worry and the fact that Suzuki was gone. Killed. By *his* hands. He couldn't think past the gentle hand on his hair, the comfort it brought. Kiku was his oldest friend.

"Try to get some sleep now, Ryu." Kiku ruffled his hair.

"I'm too scared to sleep." Indeed, his eyes wanted to close but his mind was assaulted with horrid images. Images of Nat being shot, stabbed, lying dead in a pool of blood.

"The things you're seeing in your mind will not happen, little friend." Kiku lifted Ryu off his leg to the pillows and settled in next to him.

Ryu released a sigh as Kiku's arms closed around him, a strong cocoon of warmth. He sighed and let his eyes flutter closed. Why did he always want a big strong guy to hold him? It made him such a baby, but he couldn't help it, couldn't prevent the warm strength from making him feel safe enough to sleep...

* * * *

Nat brought Seinalloy with him for backup, leaving the rest of his unit outside with the police. Several hours later after a shuttle flight to Bangkok, the Thai Royal Police escorted them to Tongmee's house. As before, Nat had the police surround the house quietly and Seinalloy wait by the door as he knocked.

Tongmee's mother answered. Her eyes went wide as soon as she saw Nat. "He's not here," she said. But the panting sound of her breath told Nat otherwise.

"He's here. Don't make me barge in. Stand aside." He cocked the safety of his gun and gently shoved Tongmee's mother out of the way.

The older woman covered her mouth with both hands and began to cry.

The altar was in the living room of the bungalow. Nat brandished his gun and moved slowly, deliberately in that direction. "Tongmee," he said softly, his heart pumping, "Put your hands up."

No answer.

Nat stopped at the doorway to the living room. He had to be extra careful. Tongmee wasn't only fierce. He was fast as hell. "Please, Tongmee. Don't make me use my gun."

Still no answer.

Nat pointed the gun through the doorway.

A foot came out like a lightning bolt and kicked the weapon from his hand. On instinct, Nat pulled back. His fists came up and the second he saw a human form he landed a punch.

Tongmee stumbled back, knocking over a table of photographs, but caught himself quickly and delivered another kick. This one caught Nat in the leg.

Nat grunted and lunged for Tongmee. He caught the slimmer man in a clinch and brought his knee into Tongmee's groin. More than anger or self-preservation fuelled his attack. Nat felt the heat in his own blood as he and Tongmee remained in their clinch, kicking and punching. Tongmee had tried to get Ryu killed. Ryu. His sweet little Ryu.

Nat lunged, shoving Tongmee back.

The room was suddenly flooded with police. Seinalloy grabbed Tongmee from behind and helped Nat wrestle him to the ground. In moments, they had him tightly pinned and handcuffed.

"He deserved it," Tongmee muttered, though blood poured from cuts on his face over his lips.

"No one deserves what you did to him." Nat held back from kicking the man in the ribcage. Rage poured through him and he forced himself not to assault Tongmee while the bastard was defenceless.

In the background, his mother screamed and wailed, but she went ignored as Seinalloy hauled Tongmee to his feet and with the aid of the officers, dragged him out of the house.

Panting heavily, his body throbbing from Tongmee's kicks and punches, Nat followed them out. He made sure Tongmee was delivered to headquarters for imprisonment. He'd await trial there and no doubt, get put away for a long time.

After hours of paperwork and processing, Nat got into a cab. His bruises were aching and screaming with pain to the touch, but he didn't care. He just wanted to get back to Phuket.

He managed to doze on the shuttle back to Phuket but he stared out the window of the taxi all the way back to Deena's house. He wanted nothing more than to slip into bed with Ryu and hold him and sleep for about five years straight. Yet, another nagging feeling weighed on him, bringing with it a sense of darkness, the way he felt in the years after Aran died. Like he'd never feel happy again, no matter what.

Truthfully, what was he expecting? For Ryu to transfer his emotions from Fujimara to him after only a couple of days and some sex? Fujimara had been his friend, lover, you name it since Ryu was a kid. Realistically, knowing how long he, himself, had been friends with Deena, it took a long time to form such bonds with a person. It didn't happen overnight. Even though he'd already thought of Ryu as 'his little Ryu.' Wishful thinking.

Even if Ryu could transfer his love that way, there was still the fact that he was basically a prostitute. He had sex with men for money. Probably lots of men. Ryu was sensuous and intensely beautiful. No doubt in Nat's mind that even Suzuki, crazy fucker that he'd been, had been drawn to Ryu's innocence and sensuality. Who wouldn't be?

Except for Fujimara. And he too, had succumbed at one point.

The taxi pulled up in front of Deena's. Nat paid the driver and got out. At this time of day, Deena and Marco would both be working. Which meant that Ryu had been alone with Fujimara for hours.

His heartbeat sped up as he mounted the steps to the front door of Deena's bungalow. He went in and stood in the entryway, listening.

Silence.

Slowly, he went towards the back, towards the spare bedroom where Ryu had been put. The door was halfway open and only quiet emanated from the room.

Quietly, Nat stepped to the doorway and peeked in. The first thing he saw was Fujimara, lying on the bed, eyes closed. He was asleep.

And Ryu was cuddled up in Fujimara's arms, asleep. One hand was curled over the larger man's biceps, as if he were hanging onto him for survival.

Nat exhaled softly. He raked a hand through his hair. Amazing how dark life could feel even when the good guys won.

He turned and trudged into Deena's living room. Sinking onto the couch, he rubbed his bruised cheek and sat back, staring up at the ceiling. Really, he wanted to leave, to go back to Bangkok and get on with his life now that he'd seen what he needed to see. But he couldn't. He'd promised Ryu he'd come back and he at least needed to wait until Ryu woke up and saw he'd kept his promise to return.

And then he'd leave.

Chapter Thirteen

Nat's eyes popped open. Someone was breathing near him. The sound teased at the edges of his nerves, showing him that his sleep had been shallow, the unsatisfying rest of someone on the edge.

He blinked and rubbed his eyes. His consciousness focusing, he felt the stiffness in his muscles, still in the same sitting position on Deena's couch. His blurred gaze caught a pair of legs next to him on the cushions. Baggy pants. Ryu's. He looked up. Ryu sat close to him, wearing his pants but no shirt. The room around them was shadowy, lit only by a few candles. That had to be Deena's work. She loved candles.

"Nat, thank God." Ryu's dark eyes were sleepy but churning with relief and worry. "I was so worried I could barely sleep."

You managed to do okay in Fujimara's arms. Nat caught himself before he said it out loud. Through his haze of exhaustion, he remembered to have sympathy. Ryu had just come from a terrifying situation. He could have been killed. And then, he'd killed a man with his bare hands. Pretty ironic considering all the protection he'd been under.

He sat up and rubbed his neck, ignoring the deep-seated impulse to pull Ryu into his arms.

"Nat, you're hurt. Let me get a cloth to put on the bruise." He started to rise.

"Don't bother, Ryu."

Ryu stopped. "Are you sure?"

"Yeah. Just sit down and relax."

Ryu obeyed and sat, looking at him.

"How are you now?" Nat asked. He remembered how Ryu had called himself a murderer and that concerned him.

Ryu frowned and Nat could see the disappointment in his eyes. "Better, I guess. I'm just so relieved you're back safe." He looked down. "Tongmee could have killed you."

Nat let himself reach out and give Ryu's shoulder a squeeze. "I've dealt with worse. Tongmee was where Kikuchiya said he was." He shook his head. "He's pretty psychic, huh?"

Ryu nodded. "Yes. He has visions all the time and stuff like that."

"Has he always been that way?"

"Since I've known him he has."

Nat raked a hand through his hair and leaned back. "Where is he now?"

"He went with Deena to bring back food for supper."

He nodded, hating that he just wanted to grab onto Ryu and tug him into the bedroom, now that they were alone. But even if he hadn't been cautious about the situation with Fujimara, he was still exhausted and felt tension now between him and Ryu. Studying Ryu's face, he felt deep concern. There hadn't been time before to consider what actually had happened while Ryu was Suzuki's prisoner. A shudder passed down his spine. "Suzuki...he didn't..." he trailed off, unable to say the word.

"If you mean, did he rape me again, then no. He didn't."
Ryu's eyes looked pained and he kept his gaze averted. He
shifted in his seat and grimaced. "He was squeezing the shit
out of my dragon, though. And then he was biting me.
Here." He pointed to one nipple. "That's when I...did the
fatal pressure point thing."

"You know about those?"

"Kiku showed me a few things way back when. Right after
the rape." Ryu's shoulders slumped, conveying his misery. "I
wish I hadn't known."

Nat stared at him. Poor Ryu really felt horrible about what
he'd done in spite of the fact that Suzuki had brutalized him
physically and emotionally more than once. Without
thinking, he reached out and smoothed back Ryu's hair. "I'm
sure as hell glad you knew. It gave me time to find
you...alive."

Ryu made eye contact now. He seemed really glad for Nat's
hand on his hair. "Thanks for saying that. It helps."

Nat caressed his hair again, feeling a bit of the tension
between them drain. "I mean it."

Ryu leaned back, his gaze still on Nat. "What'll happen
with Tongmee now?"

Nat heaved a sigh and continued to caress Ryu's hair. The
simple contact was comforting and he wished so much that
the obstacles between them didn't exist. That little bubble of
freedom from the outside they'd had for a couple of days had
now burst, letting in a gush of reality. "Well, he's in a holding
cell down at headquarters awaiting trial. Which will happen
in the next few days. No doubt, he'll end up in prison. His
career is over."

Suddenly, Ryu's hand was on his arm. "Nat, what did I do
to him to make him hate me so much?" Ryu's eyes looked

wide and mournful at the same time and he sounded like a little boy.

"You didn't do a thing. His mind was twisted. His brother died of AIDS recently and he's not dealing with it. It's my fault for keeping him on the job when I knew he was in distress."

Ryu looked at him. "Nat, you couldn't have possibly known he would go so far."

He sighed again. "That's true. If I'd thought for a second he was capable of hurting you, I'd have gotten rid of him immediately." He returned Ryu's gaze. The sweet look in the other man's eyes made an ache inside him, reminded him starkly of the barriers between them. "In any case, you're free now to go home."

The smile drained from Ryu's lips and eyes. He stared at Nat but remained silent and Nat sensed he'd said absolutely the wrong thing again.

Nat steeled himself against that wounded puppy look. What was Ryu thinking? That after two days they were going to make a life together? Ryu was naïve. Were all rent boys that naïve? Did Ryu think he'd be able to stop prostituting himself just like that and commit to one guy? And what about Fujimara? Maybe he and Ryu weren't lovers, but well, they still looked pretty cozy. And why did he even think this might be the course of Ryu's thoughts? Why was this the course of his own thoughts?

No. They were both drained and muddled and stressed. Ryu had just killed a man in self-defence. The guy had been assaulting him in a horrible way and Ryu was freaked, disoriented, and probably many other things. The best thing for him was to go home and get his life back, now that he was safe. "What's wrong? Aren't you glad?"

Ryu wished the ground would swallow him up. Somehow hearing that he was free to go home now had not been what he'd expected.

But why had he expected anything else? Was it because of the way Nat had looked at him? Held him? Devoured him during incredible, mind-blowing, passionate sex?

Ryu sighed. For a few seconds during their conversation, he'd felt lifted out of the emotional black hole he'd fallen into. Now, he was plummeting back down. Bad karma. Must be what it was. Killing Suzuki had really been a bad thing to do. He should have let the guy squeeze his cock and waited for the cops to come...

"Nothing's wrong, Nat. You're right. I'm free. And I've got a hotel to run. Kiku can't do it alone. Yuzo is a good guy but he always runs out of stuff. Green onions, miso, saké. Or he just sticks it in a corner of the fridge where you can't find it again and it rots." He was babbling now but couldn't stop himself. He wanted to maintain the composure and dignity of a White Tiger. He worked so damn hard to do it and succeeded most of the time. But he couldn't do it now. "I guess I'll go home tomorrow. Kiku can't be away from there for long." He wished Nat would stop him, shut him up with a kiss, but the big jerk was just sitting there, staring at him, full lips slightly parted.

This wasn't going well. Not at all and now he realised one of the other reasons he'd always limited sex to the White Tiger practices, to giving a bit of pleasure to a few hard-working middle-aged men. Sex just complicated everything. Especially when your heart was involved. The way it had always been involved with Kiku. "You know, I hate always having to go around the corner and bother Hojo for things in between orders, you know, because Yuzo is terrible with inventory."

Nat was still staring, his hands hanging in his lap and Ryu just wanted the guy to reach out and hug him, just so he wouldn't have to fill this uncomfortable space with his nonsense. Of course, he could just tell Nat how he felt, how taken he was with him, how their sex was the most incredible beautiful experience he'd had since he'd been with Kiku, and better in some ways because Nat made him feel much more desired than Kiku had.

But he didn't. After years and years of loving Kiku and his love being unrequited and then having his heart broken, he couldn't bear the mere thought that Nat might tell him the same thing. Especially now, when he was more raw than an uncooked piece of meat.

Just then the front door opened and Ryu heard voices. One male and one female. Deena's voice, saying something about someone and Kiku laughing. They both stopped when their gazes fell on Ryu and Nat.

Deena smiled right at him, giving Ryu the sense she had a little crush on him. "Hey cutie pie. How are you?" She set down the bundle she carried and went right over to him. To his own surprise, he didn't feel uncomfortable at all with her attention, the way she took his hand and put a wrist against his forehead. "I always check for fever. Don't mind me. Cool as a cucumber."

He returned her smile, kind of liking her fussing. "I'm okay."

She pulled back and looked at him and he could see the doubt in her eyes. He remembered what Nat had said about her powers of observation. "If you say so, honey. But I think you need more rest and more loving care." He saw Deena throw a glance at Nat.

By this time, Kiku had approached him, also carrying a bundle, his expression concerned. "I'm worried about you, too."

Ryu shrugged. He wasn't about to tell them out in the open how Nat's comment had blown a hole through his middle. "I'm fine. Kind of ironic, don't you think? You were all so worried about my safety and after all this time I'm the one who did Suzuki in with my bare hands?"

Kiku frowned. "That doesn't mean you no longer need worry or care."

He stood up. "I'll put on a shirt and then come help with the food." Before they could protest, he headed towards the bedroom, painfully aware of how Nat had remained silent all this time.

Sitting next to Ryu at the table, listening to Deena and Kiku's lively conversation, Nat realised one of the reasons he'd stayed out of romantic entanglements. Aside from the reason that his heart had always been locked away, it was this messy stuff that had stopped him, this feeling jealous and needing and wanting someone, then worrying about losing them, whether it was because of a psychopathic maniac or because the guy was so hot, you just knew he'd end up in other men's arms anyway. It sucked.

Ryu had been sitting quietly close by, taking a small bite of his food now and then and contributing to the conversation when addressed. Every so often their gazes met and then Ryu looked away.

"Ryu, sweetie, aren't you hungry?" Deena was looking at Ryu again in that sympathetic way. Nat knew his friend well. She was happily married, but it didn't stop her from having a sort of crush-maternal thing going on with Ryu.

Understandable. To be in Ryu's presence for a few minutes was to be taken with him in some way.

Ryu shook his head and took a sip of tea. His chopsticks sat across the top of his bowl. "No, thanks, Deena. I'm sorry. I know you went to a lot of trouble."

"No trouble, honey."

Ryu smiled at her. "And thank you for everything. I really appreciate it. I'll miss you when Kiku and I leave tomorrow."

Deena's eyes widened and Nat felt his stomach jump. "You're leaving so soon?" she asked.

"Don't you need a bit more time to rest?" Fujimara asked. Nat saw the pointed look the older man was giving him. And he saw Ryu ignore it.

"I feel rested enough. Better to get back to our lives."

Fujimara nodded. "All right. We have clearance to return on any flight we wish."

A breeze passed through the open window, rustling some nearby palm trees. This was a nice place. He and Nat had some really sweet times packed into a couple of days. He'd just have to take the memories back to Tokyo with him. Because he was waiting for Nat to say, "Don't go. Stay here with me," and Nat wasn't saying a word.

Hurt spiked through him. He'd gotten attached to Kiku in pretty much the same way. Hard and fast.

"I'll miss you too, Ryu."

Ryu looked at Deena, as if she'd voiced what he wanted Nat to say. "I hope you'll come visit us. You and Marco can stay at the White Tiger as long as you want, complimentary. Right, Kiku?"

"Of course."

Ryu got up and picked up his bowl. "I'll help clean up."

"You will not." Deena reached over and took the bowl from his hands. "Go rest, relax, do whatever it is you need to."

He looked at her. This being an honoured guest kind of thing was alien to him. "Are you sure?"

Deena smiled. "I'm positive." She got up and came around to him, wrapping him in a warm hug. She was soft but he couldn't help wishing it was Nat holding him. Deena smelled like perfume and Ryu already craved Nat's clean, male, no-nonsense scent.

"If you fall asleep and I don't see you after this, have a safe trip home." Deena released him and stood back.

"Thank you." He looked at Kiku and then at Nat. Which one of them would stay in the room with him tonight? They were both looking at him in silence, as if expecting him to decide something.

He sighed. How ironic. He'd railed against feeling so powerless over his own life and finally, when he had a choice, that was when he really needed Nat to take the initiative.

Fuck it.

"I'm going to shower," he said, and turned without another word.

"Nat, can I talk with you in the kitchen?" Deena was glaring at him and he had the feeling he was in for a tongue-lashing.

Nat glanced at Fujimara who sat, head bowed, saying nothing. Strange response, considering that Ryu was about to be naked and wet a short distance away. If Fujimara was feeling what *he* was feeling, then it would require getting up and joining Ryu in the bathroom. But Deena was waiting. "Sure." He followed her into the kitchen.

Where she turned on him. "What the hell, Nat? What did you say to Ryu while we were out? He looked so upset. And don't tell me it's only because of what he's been through. I know better than that."

He sighed and raked a hand through his hair. "I told him he was free to go home now."

Deena threw up her hands. "I can't believe you! The poor cutie pie." She shook her head and crossed her arms. "Nat, I love you with all my heart, you know that, but really, you can be so thick. He's crazy about you. And I *know* it's mutual."

Nat put his hands on his hips and glanced over his shoulder. No doubt, Fujimara could hear their conversation...and even though he didn't speak Thai, he'd no doubt guess from their tones of voice what the conversation was about...well, if he hadn't already gotten up and gone into the bathroom. "It's not that simple, Deena. You don't know the whole story."

Deena cocked her head. She always did that when she was really annoyed. "I'm not sure I need to, Nat. You know, Marco and I are happy together, and there have been problems, but we worked them out. What can be a stickier problem than what I've gone through? Marco is straight and I didn't...go through with the whole thing. He deals with it."

Nat stared at her. "You didn't do the gender reassignment surgery?"

She shook her head. "No." Then an almost shy look came into her eyes, along with a tiny smile. Totally uncharacteristic for Deena. "It's better this way. Now I can offer the best of not just both worlds, but *all* worlds." Then she turned fully and shook her finger at him. "I'm making a point here. You don't just let go of a guy like Ryu, no matter what. He's special."

He bowed his head. "I know."

"Look, you're a grown man and I'm not one to tell anyone else what to do. I just care about you, and I know what you've been through. I'll leave it at that. For now. Okay?"

"Yes, ma'am."

Finally Deena smiled. She'd never been able to sustain being pissed at either him or Aran. "Now get out of the kitchen. Maybe you have someone to check up on."

He grinned at her in spite of his dark feeling. "Yes, ma'am."

As he left the kitchen, he met Fujimara coming in with some dishes. Nat's gut lurched. The other man had a strange look on his face but he smiled, a charming kind of look that made Nat begin to understand why Ryu had been taken with him. At least Ryu had excellent taste. Fujimara was...well, for lack of another word, hot. It made Nat feel complimented. Ryu apparently had a thing for big masculine guys.

"Kikuchiya," Deena said in English, "I'm sending Nat to check up on Ryu. What do you think?"

Fujimara nodded. "Yes, Ryu would like that." He smiled at Nat, and Nat couldn't sense any possessiveness in the other man.

Well, the guy probably didn't need to be insecure, knowing how devoted Ryu was to him. The situation was weird, made Nat feel as if he'd taken some kind of hallucinogenic that was skewing his perception. In any case, for this moment, he had a chance to be alone with Ryu, and found that moth-to-light irresistible pull Ryu had on him.

Nat headed towards the bathroom, his heart pounding.

The shower was off and the louver door slid partway open. Ryu wasn't in there.

Nat turned to the other side of the tiny hallway. The bedroom door was closed. Taking a deep breath, he knocked.

After a few seconds it opened. Ryu stood there, his hips wrapped in a fluffy towel. His hair was wet, a shiny ebony and stood in a spiky wildness. His eyes widened a bit. "Hi."

Nat looked down. As much as he was captured by Ryu's colourful, lickable torso, he felt like he shouldn't be staring. "Hey. Can I come in?"

Wordlessly, Ryu stepped aside and closed the door behind him. Then he stood there, silent. Well, Nat figured he was only getting his own silence back.

"I…um…came to check up on you. I was worried. How's your…dragon?"

A small, humourless chuckle escaped Ryu. "It's a bit sore, but otherwise functional."

"Can I see?" The question popped out before Nat could stop it. Actually, in truth, he *did* want to see Ryu's cock, and not just to make sure it was okay. "I…want to make sure."

Ryu was smiling, though the humour didn't quite reach his eyes. The expression in them was that tentative yet hopeful look Nat had seen before. "I didn't know you were a physician too."

"I'm not."

"I knew that." He pulled off the towel and held his hands out wide. "Well, here it is."

Nat pulled in a soft breath. His heart sped up its pumping, sending blood right into his cock. He gestured towards the bed. "Go sit down, so I can take a proper look."

"Nat, you don't have to do this. If it's not what you really want, I'd just as soon go to sleep."

"I do want to. Please, Ryu."

Ryu's look shifted, softened. "Okay." He went to the bed and sank down.

Nat knelt down and with gentle hands on Ryu's knees, opened his thighs so he could kneel between them. He heard

Ryu's breath catch. "I want to make sure you're not injured," he said softly.

Ryu's cock was kind of in the halfway hard point. Interesting, considering it had been hanging there soft when he'd first opened the towel. Gingerly, Nat reached out and brushed several fingertips over the head and then down the straightening shaft, earning a harsh exhale from Ryu.

He pulled back. "Did that hurt?"

Ryu shook his head. "No." His voice was a bit deeper, huskier now. "But check it again, just to be sure."

Nat glanced up at him. Ryu's beautiful eyes were dusky, the lids heavy.

He reached out again, this time letting Ryu's cock rest in his palm. He glided his thumb along the silky skin, over the hardness and veins. The reddish shaft made his mouth begin to water. "Still all right?"

"Yeah." Ryu's chest was rising and falling more heavily. "Nat," he whispered. "Maybe you should taste it."

Nat's insides jumped. Ryu's cock surged in his hand as if agreeing with the suggestion. "You're right." He leaned forward, enveloped by Ryu's sandalwood aroma and licked Ryu's cock, a gentle slide of his tongue from base to head.

"Ohhh." Ryu's hand came out and nestled in the top of his hair, fingers agitating. "That's good."

Desire, like liquid heat in his veins, spread through Nat's whole body. Whatever hesitations he had fell to the side. He knew in the back of his mind he'd pick them up later, but right now, he had his own special first aid to administer.

Leaning over Ryu's groin, he took that delicious cock all the way in. One firm slide and he'd swallowed Ryu to the base. Damn, nothing had ever tasted better to him in his whole life. Like it had before, the world spun away, and all that existed was Ryu's flavour and texture, the grip of his fingers in Nat's hair and the tiny pleasure noises he was making with each dip and suck that Nat gave him.

Without thinking, Nat lifted away and gently pushed Ryu onto his back. A fever to taste Ryu everywhere gripped him, like fire through a brush. With his hands on Ryu's thighs, he spread him open and licked every spot he could find.

The first place he lavished with his tongue was Ryu's firm balls. With the flat of his tongue he savoured every rounded contour, glad that Ryu was lying there, whispering his name and groaning with enjoyment. Nat knew that afterward, he'd wonder about how many guys Ryu had let do this to him, but for now, all he wanted was more.

He slid his hands up Ryu's thighs to his hard ass, lifting him up so he could get to every spot. He worked his way downward over Ryu's perineum and found the tight bud of his opening with the tip of his tongue.

"Oh, yes!" Ryu breathed in between panting gasps. All his enjoyment did was make Nat feel wilder. He stayed where he was and licked and sucked until he was sure he heard Ryu begging him for more.

When he looked up, Ryu had lifted his head. "Nat, please." He sat up and was clutching at Nat's jeans.

Just for tonight, Ryu said in his fevered mind. Maybe Nat didn't want him for more than this, but at least he could have some fantasies to take back to Tokyo. His hands scrabbled at Nat's jeans and he got them open while Nat lifted off his T-shirt. Nat's cock stood up in a hard curve from his muscular body and just the sight made Ryu want it buried deep inside his ass. He didn't bother with the oil. It was somewhere in his bag that had been rescued from the gym by one of the agents and Ryu didn't want to take the time.

He spit into his hand and lathered Nat's thick delicious dragon up before pulling Nat down on top of him. He loved being on his back and having Nat's large body cover his, fill the space between his thighs with his powerful form.

Clutching Nat's back with one hand, he wrapped his legs around Nat's hips and guided the head of Nat's cock to his aching hole. Nat was busy kissing him, sliding his tongue, hot and moist around Ryu's as if tasting the most delicious meal.

Who cared? As long as he got that dragon into its cave.

Nat moaned when the head of his cock poked in. Ryu grabbed at his back and pulled Nat in deeper. Sparks exploded in his mind as that thick cock stretched his ass, filled him with delicious hardness.

Nat's hand brushed back over his hair. The movement was so tender, so passionate, hard to believe it was the same man who could say such dumb things and remain silent the way he did. As Nat pumped into him, one firm stroke after the next, each burst of pleasure made another memory surface. Nat defending him from Tongmee, helping him out of his trauma, comforting him after his phone call with Kiku, telling him how beautiful he was.

Ryu pulled Nat closer, kissed him with a passionate chafing of their lips together. This was the man who'd wanted him. If he wasn't telling Ryu to stay in Thailand, there *had* to be a good reason. Ryu had to believe that. And be content with the heat between them in this moment. It was never a good idea to want more than what life gave you.

Nat rammed into him. That thick cock rubbed his prostate. The sparks went to the head of his dragon, made more intense by the rub of Nat's belly on it as their bodies chafed together. Ryu squeezed his eyes shut, head tilted back, his mouth open, slack, accepting Nat's deep hot kisses.

Nat braced himself on his elbows and drove in harder. The sweat on his skin glistened and dropped onto Ryu. *Nat.* The name spiraled through his mind, over and over as Nat rode him. Hot, sweaty, slamming together. The pressure was cresting hard and fast and on the next slam, Ryu exploded. His cum shot between them.

The release was long and intense, waves that made him groan into Nat's mouth. Time and space melted, condensed into the climax gripping his body. He clenched his hands on Nat's ass, pulling him, urging him on. He squeezed his muscles around Nat's cock. Nat's answering groan vibrated into his mouth. Another slide and Ryu felt the warm eruption filling his passage.

He held on to Nat until the larger man's body went slack and then pulled Nat down on top of him. He closed his eyes, breathing in Nat's scent and the musk of their sex, loving the heat of Nat's sweatymuscles fused to his.

Deep sadness immediately filled the aftermath. Ryu squeezed Nat tightly, hoping the thick-headed guy would at least get the message and stay the night with him. Apparently he did, for as soon as he'd gently rolled off of Ryu, insisted on cleaning him up and used the bathroom, he padded back in and pulled Ryu against him, spooning him in the warm curve of his hard body. Of course, Nat didn't say anything and Ryu wondered if he was normally this quiet. He was used to someone like Kiku who was very verbal, always chatting with guests and explaining about the White Tiger path to him and the others, and who always tried to give an answer other than silence.

Unlike Nat.

He sighed, feeling his back move against Nat's broad chest. He wasn't sure if Nat was sleeping but didn't say anything, and eventually felt his own exhaustion take over. Tomorrow there was one last chance for Nat to say something, something to let Ryu know that maybe, just maybe, these last couple of days held the promise of something more.

Why was he even thinking like this? It was his nature, he guessed. Even in his worst moments, there had always been something in him that had never given up, that had wanted to know the world held better things than what he'd suffered. And life had responded. Kiku had been there, even with all his faults.

Yeah, tomorrow, he'd wait and see if Nat took that one last chance. And then, if he didn't, Ryu would go back to Tokyo.

Chapter Fourteen

Something warm and soft on his face woke Nat up. He opened his eyes and saw the curtain wafting in the breeze from the open window. Ryu was still in his arms, asleep, his breath rising and falling gently. A sweet sound.

He heaved a sigh. That dark feeling he'd gone to sleep with was still there. Except for one thing. The nightmare. It hadn't woken him up. Damn. For the first time since Aran had died, Nat's dreams hadn't been full of that horrid memory, waking him up in a sweat. Ryu was curled up against him, fitting perfectly in his embrace, as he had seemed to fit from the first time.

The dark feeling became an ache. Words rose to his lips, hovered there, almost driving him to nudge Ryu awake and tell him everything he felt.

No. All the reasons that wedged between them were still there, stark in the morning light. The image of Ryu's hand clutching Fujimara's arm in his sleep was burned in Nat's mind. Ryu's true feelings coming out in his unconscious state.

How long would it be until Ryu realised how he felt and went running back to Tokyo anyway?

Ryu stirred. He was obviously waking up and Nat felt the last of their moments slipping away. Ryu's eyes opened, sleepy and sweet. He stared up at Nat. One hand rested on Nat's shoulder. Ryu seemed to be waiting.

Nat leaned down and pressed a soft kiss to his lips. "What time is your flight?"

The pain fleeting through Ryu's face made him wince. "Soon. I should get up." He said that but then stayed where he was, though his hand slipped off Nat's arm. "Nat."

Nat's heart jumped. "Yeah?"

"We had a nice time, didn't we?"

That ache in his chest tightened a moment. He brushed his fingertips across Ryu's cheek. "Yes. Really nice."

Ryu covered his hand, just for a second and then lifted Nat's hand away. Without another word, he pushed back the covers and got out of the bed. Nat watched him wrap a towel around his hips and go to the bathroom. Then he heard the shower go on.

He suppressed a smile. Ryu had a compulsion about showering. One of the things that made him so...incredible. He sighed.

* * * *

An hour later, Ryu zipped his bag and stood. He still wanted Nat to stop him, to give him *some* indication that he...wanted...him. A word. A gesture.

But nothing. What the hell? It was as if that incredible heat between them had never happened. He was on the verge of asking Nat what the hell his problem was. No. He wasn't even going there. He wasn't putting his heart out on the ground in front of Nat and giving the guy a chance to stomp on it.

Kiku appeared behind Nat. "The taxi is here."

Ryu's heart sped up. His stomach twisted up. Here was the last chance. He went to the door and stood in front of him. Nat's potent maleness shimmered off him. The scent of him started to make Ryu dizzy. He waited.

Still nothing. Instead, he stood aside, letting Ryu pass by him.

Ryu followed Kiku out of Deena's house, towards the idling cab. He was vividly aware of Nat behind him, all the way out to the street. Again, he turned and faced Nat, sensing emotions and thoughts roiling in the other man. But he couldn't make sense of Nat's turmoil any more than he could of his own. Perhaps if he hadn't just killed someone with his bare hands while the guy was squeezing the life out of his privates, he would have been clearer.

As it was, he desperately needed Nat to make the first move.

Unfortunately, Nat's only move was to do and say nothing.

"Agent Phoenix, thank you for taking care of Ryu." Kiku bowed to him.

Nat returned the gesture. "You're welcome, even though I did a lousy job of it."

Kiku grinned. "I know the feeling. Anyway, take care." He turned and went into the cab, leaving Ryu with Nat.

He waited for Nat to say something, giving the man one chance after the next. Nat didn't seem to want to take any of them.

Ryu didn't fight the sting of rejection. He let it flow through him. Lifting up on his toes, he pressed a quick kiss to Nat's rugged cheek. "Bye, Nat. Thank you…for everything."

"You're welcome, Ryu. I'm sorry I didn't…do better."

Ryu furrowed his brow. What exactly was Nat referring to? Well, he wasn't going to wait for an answer that hurt even worse than the silence. "It's okay." Without another word, he got into the cab and closed the door.

The driver pulled away from Deena's house and Ryu glanced back just for a second. Nat was standing there, watching the taxi, but he didn't wave and Ryu began to doubt whether the other man had even seen him look back.

He turned and sat back with a deep sigh. He stiffened when his gaze met Kiku's. His friend had that look he got when he was about to tell Ryu his insights. "Kiku, I beg you, don't say anything, okay? I have some insight too and, well, no matter what's going on in Nat's mind, there are times you just need a person to get over it and *do* something. You know."

Kiku grinned, though his eyes remained sympathetic. "Ryu. I *do* have something else to tell you. There just hasn't been a chance until now. Is that all right?"

His stomach tightened. "What is it?"

"A few hours after I spoke with your father and Hayao Suzuki, your father sent an envelope of money to the White Tiger. There was more in there than I'd ever paid to Suzuki in extortion. And there was this note with it." Kiku pulled out a white slip of paper.

Ryu's heart sped up. "My father wrote a note?"

Kiku nodded. "Would you like to read it?"

Feeling suddenly weak, he shook his head. "Read it to me, please? Only if I'll be glad."

Kiku gave a brief nod. "I think you'll be somewhat glad." He opened the folds of paper. "Kiku-san, I'll never be able to make up to my son for what he suffered. Please take this as a gesture for you and for him, to use as you see fit. It's not a substitute for what I should have given but is what I have at this time. From now on, if anyone tries to harm Ryu or anyone connected with you or him, I'll make sure justice is done. In any case, you have my complete protection. You will never have to walk the streets of Tokyo in fear. Naboru Miyazaki."

Ryu stared. Hot tears bit at his eyes. "Did he really write that?"

Kiku folded the paper and stuck it in his bag. "Of course, Ryu. I wouldn't make it up for effect."

"I know that. It's just…hard to believe." A tear rolled onto his cheek. He brushed it away and forced the rest of them back. "It's…enough, I suppose."

A smile played about Kiku's lips. He reached forward and his large hand closed over Ryu's and squeezed. "My beautiful friend, it could never be enough. Not all the money in the world, not all the love in the world. He'd need a thousand lifetimes to make up for what you suffered." His hand rested another moment on Ryu's then slipped away and he sat back. "It's enough however, to show you that people can do and say the right things given some time."

Ryu looked at him. His friend returned his stare but didn't say anything else.

* * * *

Two weeks later…

Damn, Ryu felt so good. Nat pushed his cock deep inside that tight, delicious passage and Ryu's ass swallowed him to the hilt. Ryu's colourful body was slick with sweat and the squeeze of those hands on his ass cheeks was heaven itself.

"Yes, Nat. Ohhh!" Ryu threw his head back, lips parted. He squeezed that ring of muscles in his ass around Nat's cock, making him groan...

Nat opened his eyes. He heard heavy breathing, then realised it was his own. Damn, he was alone. Like before. Before Ryu.

He heaved a deep sigh. The slight lift of his back against the sheets made him feel the sweat pouring over his body and the rigid, swollen state of his cock.

And the ache in his chest.

He stared up at the ceiling. His apartment in Bangkok was never really dark and the walls were too thin. Lights from the streetlamps and car headlights brightened his room and even distant traffic and people noises filtered in. Phuket had been so quiet in comparison. All he'd heard then was Ryu's quiet breathing next to him.

He sat up and went to pee, but stood there unsuccessful, was too fucking hard to piss and didn't want to jack off. That just held no appeal. It might release the tension in his cock...his...dragon, Ryu had called it, but then the ache would only get worse. Someone...Ryu...had really made his cock get connected to his heart in a way it hadn't ever been. It was because of Ryu he'd even *begun* to deal with his feelings about Aran. Probably was no accident that the nightmares had finally stopped after all this time.

Nat turned on the shower, stripped off his boxers and stepped under the cold spray. The water jolted him but he stood there, taking the icy battering almost as punishment for letting Ryu believe he didn't want him. Damn, just the image of Ryu's kissing his cheek and then climbing into the taxi to leave made him wince. And then, instead of righting the wrong, he'd stood there like a dumbass and watched the cab roll away. Deena had been right to call him an idiot when she came home and found out what happened.

How had this happened? In a few days? Impossible. But here he was. Unable to sleep because he missed that guy too much, and his arms physically ached to hold him. The water grew warmer and Nat soaped up a washcloth and scrubbed his skin, as if he could wash his ache out.

It didn't work. Suddenly, all the arguments he'd posed in his head meant shit. *Ryu was a prostitute. Ryu did this kind of thing with a lot of men. Ryu was really in love with Kiku.* It was all bullshit, true or not. Nothing was worth a shit here when life had grown darker because Ryu was back in Tokyo.

Nat rinsed and turned the shower knobs to 'off.' He grabbed a towel and dried himself while his decision formed and solidified. He threw his toiletries into his shaving kit and then stuffed it into his duffel, along with some changes of clothes and Aran's small favourite Buddha statue, then left his apartment, locking the door behind him. He could call into headquarters and tell them of his emergency leave of absence while he was in the cab to the airport.

* * * *

"You ran out of green onions again, Yuzo." Ryu sighed and shut the door of the giant stainless steel refrigerator.

Yuzo's face crumpled. "I'm sorry."

Ryu looked at the guy. The same guy who'd made sure all the agents had known where to find him so they could rescue him. The same guy who'd offered to stay on the phone with him so he wouldn't feel so frightened and alone and who'd told him where to find Suzuki's gun. So far, Yuzo was all right.

He smiled and put a hand on Yuzo's shoulder. "No problem. I'll go down to Hojo's. He'll be happy to spare a few until our shipment comes." Hojo and his lover ran a bistro a few doors down and they were always generous when Yuzo ran out of ingredients.

"Are you sure?" Worry darkened Yuzo's large eyes and Ryu was beginning to understand why he had captured Kiku's heart. He was basically good. Messed up and spoiled in some ways, but as good-hearted as he was pretty. It was probably difficult not to end up spoiled when your parents were wealthy and your uncle had been a famous film and *noh* theatre actor.

He nodded. "I'm sure. Besides, it feels damn good to be able to walk around outside and not worry." *For the first time since he was seventeen.*

"Okay, but take a phone anyway. All right?" Yuzo took one of the hotel cell phones that he kept in his pocket and handed it to him.

Ryu accepted the offering and felt a flush of warmth towards Yuzo. Kiku's boyfriend was turning out to be somewhat of a mother hen, and it was kinda nice. A bit like Nat's friend Deena. And Yuzo made good soup too.

Letting the sudden ache pass through him, he went to the front door, slipped on his thong sandals and went out.

Down at Hojo's, Hojo and his boyfriend both fussed over Ryu while they got the green onions for him and handed him the plastic bag. Though the attention was nice, Ryu couldn't ignore the ache that seemed to be with him all the time now, sitting in his chest like a rock. He sighed as he walked back towards the White Tiger. It just seemed to be his lot. A few sweet times with his dream men and then the rest of the time he was to be of service to old guys like Mr. Hamura. Well, it could be a hell of a lot worse. And had been. Quite recently.

Then the cell phone rang. Out of habit, Ryu pushed the button and put the phone to his ear. *"Moshi moshi*, White Tiger."

Nat's hand shook on the phone. That familiar sweet voice made him ache even though he was only a few feet from the entrance of the hotel. He could even see the white tigers etched into the glass of the front doors. But he hid in the cab where it idled at the curb, just until he was sure Ryu wanted him here. "Ryu?"

Pause. "Nat? Is that you?"

A sudden splash of colour caught Nat's eye. He looked out the rear window of the taxi. And saw him. Ryu had rounded the corner. He wore a white sleeveless shirt and the inked colours on his arms and shoulders flashed like neon signs. A small plastic bag of green onions hung from one hand. His hair was still all one colour. No pink tips. Somehow, Nat was glad even though his heart pounded. "Yeah. I…um…was hoping you wouldn't mind if I…came to Tokyo…to see you."

He watched Ryu freeze on the sidewalk. "You want to come here?"

"Yes. I…miss you. Is it okay?" He waited, his gaze trained on Ryu for his response. He could swear he saw Ryu's eyes light up. A small ray of hope burned.

"That's okay. When would you get here?"

Nat grinned in spite of his nervousness. "In about two seconds." He laughed at Ryu's puzzled look. "I'm right here. In the taxi at the curb." He saw Ryu scan the street and look right at him. He shut the phone off, paid the driver and got right out.

Damn it was good to see Ryu coming towards him. He squelched the urge to reach out and grab him in an embrace because Ryu's expression, though glad, still held an air of caution.

Ryu stopped in front of him and stood, staring. In one hand he clutched the phone, in the other, the sack of scallions. "Nat, I can't believe you're here." This was a busy neighbourhood, Nat noted, partly out of nervousness, just as he noticed Ryu hadn't put the nose ring back in. Cars and trucks chugged back and forth on the street and people moved around them on the sidewalk. Not even the smell of city exhaust however, could completely drown out Ryu's scent. That oil he wore. Brought back great memories. Nat hoped to make more of those.

"Ryu, I acted like a real asshole just before you left. I got all choked up and didn't tell you the truth."

Ryu's brow furrowed. "The truth?"

"Yeah. I don't care if you're with lots of guys or what you do. I really want —"

"You think I'm with lots of guys?" Ryu looked confused. "You mean sex?"

He nodded, heart still pounding like a jackrabbit. "Well…" He gestured towards the hotel. "After you told me more about this place."

Ryu laughed. "I don't have sex with lots of guys. I mean, I have a few regulars that Kiku handpicked because they're older and would never hurt me. But they mostly want a massage…with a…you know, happy ending." Shyness flashed through his eyes. "But that's it. I really just help Kiku run the place." He held up the plastic bag. "Like getting onions for the soup." Ryu's cheeks reddened and a light of understanding flooded his beautiful face. "You thought that…you and me…the way we were…that I did *that* all the time?"

Nat bowed his head. He'd said the wrong thing before to Ryu but now he felt like he'd stuck his foot in his mouth all the way to the knee. He heard Ryu make a huffing sound and looked up at him.

"Nat, you jerk. You should have asked me. I haven't done…what we did…in years. Not since Kiku and I…" He fell silent for a moment. "No wonder you acted that way."

Relief flooded him. Even so, he'd come here ready to deal with that if it had been true. "I'm sorry. I just get so…I don't know…nervous around you."

Ryu's eyebrows rose. "Nervous? With me?"

He nodded. "My words get all muddled up and I can't think straight."

To his surprise, Ryu's eyes lit up again and he grinned. "I'll take that as a good thing. Since you're here."

He returned the smile. "It's very good." He took a deep breath. "Anyway, you told me the other day that if I'd ever come here, you'd have wanted to be a partner with me for this…thing you do. I was hoping…I mean, whatever you'd want. I've never met anyone like you. You're…special." His tongue was tripping all over itself again, but at least he was trying to say what he meant.

Ryu's smile deepened, but suddenly faded. "What about your work?"

"I'm on an emergency leave of absence with no designated date of return." He cleared his throat. "I'm prepared to…become a boxing coach…if it's wanted." He gave Ryu what he hoped was a pointed look. "Like I say, whatever *you* want. I just missed you so much it hurt."

Ryu looked down. "I've missed you too. A lot."

"So? What do you say? You want a partner?"

His question earned another deep smile. This one was joyful and made Ryu's face shine. He shoved the phone in the pocket of his baggy pants and threw his arms around Nat.

Before Nat could say anything, Ryu went up on tiptoes and his soft lips were pressed to Nat's. Relief swept through him. Ryu felt incredible in his arms, his lips were delicious, like coming home to everything sweet after being in hell. He didn't even care that thousands of people could see them. All he felt was…happy.

Finally, Ryu broke the kiss and went back down to his feet. His eyes were dusky, his lips swollen, but there was only one word to describe his look also. *Happy.* "Come on, Nat." He picked up Nat's hand, which he gave a tug, pulling him in the direction of the glass doors with the white tigers etched in them. "I sure as hell want you to be my partner. And we can get started right now."

About the Author

Sedonia Guillone is a multi-published, award nominated author of both m/f and m/m erotic romance. The man in her life is her inspiration and provides all the hands-on research she needs. When she's not writing, she's cuddling, watching samurai flicks and thinking about the next naughty, delicious tale she wants to write.

Sedonia loves to hear from readers. You can find her contact information, website details and author profile page at http://www.total-e-bound.com.

Total-E-Bound Publishing

www.total-e-bound.com

Take a look at our exciting range of literagasmic™
erotic romance titles and discover pure quality
at Total-E-Bound.